KEEPING DENVER

SANDY ALVAREZ

CRYSTAL DANIELS

TWO PENS-

CRYSTAL *Daniels*

Sandy ALVAREZ

-ONE STORY

NOTE FROM AUTHORS

This book is a fast paced insta-love romance

1

DENVER

Holding back tears, I shiver from the blistering winter winds as I stare through the frosted laundromat window. *Fuck my life.* I've stooped to a new low. Blowing into my icy cold hands, trying to warm them, I continue to stand outside, in the cold; waiting for the woman inside to transfer her clothes from the washing machine into the dryer, hoping she will walk away and leave her clothes unattended as she has done a few times within the last two hours she's been here. I've been homeless for going on six months now, and I've been turned down from every job I've applied for. They all took one look at my threadbare t-shirt, dirty jeans, and holey sneakers, currently held together with duct tape, and turned up their judgmental noses. I've been sent packing more times than I can count, all except for one. The shithole diner I applied to a month ago. The waitressing position looked promising until the manager implied the only way I'd be getting the job was if I was willing to get down on my knees for it. I was desperate, but not enough to offer my body or self-respect. No matter how hungry, cold or on the brink of giving up I am, my body is the one thing I will never give away. Living on the streets, you see unspeakable things women and men do to survive, and I promised myself I wouldn't become one of them.

The wind whips my long red hair around my face, and my teeth chatter from the cold. Glancing down at the watch I found in a dumpster last month, I notice it's 9:05 am. My interview is at 10:30. *Shit, I'm going to be late.*

After walking away from the diner four weeks ago, I went straight to the public library. The same library I have been kicked out of on several occasions for my somewhat unkempt appearance. I hate the way people look at the homeless—with disgust. Many treat us like trash, spitting insults, or saying shit like, "Why don't you get a job and help yourself?" Just like the woman who worked at the library did to me last month when I tried to go in there and use one of their computers to search for a job and fill out applications. Did she not understand that I WAS trying to help myself? God, people are so ignorant and cruel. Lucky for me, that nasty woman wasn't working the next day when I decided to go back and try again. Instead, there was an older man, if I had to guess, somewhere in his mid-sixties. He was kind and treated me with respect. The older man who introduced himself as Roland had ignored my appearance while guiding me to one of their computer stations. He even sat down with me and helped me search for a job. Together we filled out at least a dozen applications. With only a high school diploma and not much in the way of experience except for waitressing, my options were limited. Over the next couple of weeks, I went to the library and continued my hunt.

I find it crazy that nowadays, everything is done online. Whatever happened to face-to-face interviews? I guess in my case it works out. This way, they can't judge me based on my appearance. The last day I had gone into the library, Roland, the older man, mentioned his grandson, Lucas, worked for some fancy lawyer downtown. Lucas told Roland his boss was looking for a personal assistant. Lucas had mentioned the job to his sister when they were over at Roland's house for supper earlier that week. Roland called his grandson right then and there, asking if the position was still available. His grandson confirmed it was, but I politely declined. I was in no place to be working in some classy, upscale office. Not only do I not look the part, but my computer skills are almost nonexistent. The sweet older man took down the address and phone number of the assistant job and slipped it to me anyway. He said to keep it if I changed my mind. And I'll never forget his parting words. "You may think you're not good enough for a lot of things, but trust me child, you are. And don't let a damn person tell you differently."

After two days had passed with no word from any job prospects, I bit the bullet and used the prepaid phone I saved for an entire month to purchase minutes for and called the number on a piece of paper the man at the library gave me. The nice woman I talked to didn't even ask for a resume. She sounded almost desperate to find someone, so I'm assuming that is why she hadn't bothered with asking about my experience. She'll find out soon enough, though. Now, here I am about to steal someone else's clothes to go on an interview for a job I am almost certain I won't get. I don't know the first thing about being a lawyer's assistant. I can't believe they agreed to the interview in the first place, but I am in no position to turn down any opportunity given to me.

Movement out of the corner of my eye catches my attention and brings me back to what I came here for. As expected, the woman I have been watching exits the laundromat, walks right past me, and heads to the coffee shop across the street. I shake my head at the lady. Who the hell leaves their shit unattended in a city like New York, especially in a neighborhood like this where there are dozens of people waiting to take what you have?

After watching the woman disappear inside the shop, I slip

into the laundromat and over to the pile of clothes neatly folded in the basket next to the dryer. Sifting through the pile, I come across a pair of black slacks, a soft pink blouse, and a navy blouse. I take all three items and shove them under my secondhand, worn out jacket then dart out of the laundromat. I casually look over my shoulder to make sure I wasn't spotted stealing and to see if anyone is following me.

With the coast clear, I duck into a little corner market. The cashier behind the counter eyes me suspiciously before her attention quickly diverts to the customer who has just approached her. Taking advantage of her distraction, I make my way to the back of the store to the ladies' room. When I step inside, I flip the lock on the door and tug off my backpack, setting it on the counter next to the sink. Quickly, I kick off my tennis shoes then strip out of my jeans and t-shirt. When I look in the mirror, I take in my semi-clean, red hair that hangs nearly to my waist. Next, I look at the body of a girl I don't recognize anymore. My pale skin is a stark contrast to my blue eyes that have become dull over the years.

Growing up in the foster system, you never know if the family you are placed with will feed you regularly, but never had my weight dropped this much. Never have I been this thin. I remember when I couldn't wait to turn eighteen and age out of the system. All I ever wanted was to feel free. Free from being bounced around from one home to the next. Free from the men and women who hated children but housed them to cash a check, a check that instead of being used to buy me clothes and food was used to feed a drug habit or spent on their biological children. And finally, I wanted to be free of the last home I stayed in. The Marks home had been by far the best place I had lived in years. Until six months after I turned seventeen, when Mr. Marks had started acting and looking at me in a way that caused my skin to crawl. Three months shy of my eighteenth birthday, with only a backpack full of what little belongings I owned, I walked out of what would be my final foster home and never looked back. I stayed at a shelter, and started a job working at a fast-food place where I met my co-worker, Tiffany. Tiffany had an apartment and was looking for a roommate since hers had flaked on her a few weeks before. I eagerly accepted the invitation to live with her.

We got along okay for five years. Until she met her boyfriend, Jeremy. I knew Jeremy was into some heavy stuff, meaning drugs. It didn't take long for Tiffany to follow his destructive path of drug abuse. Once she had quit her job, things started to spiral.

My job was barely covering my half of the rent and utilities, let alone Tiffany's half. Then one day after work, I came home to find the locks changed and all my belongings sitting outside the apartment. There was an eviction notice taped to the door. Apparently, Tiffany and her coked-out boyfriend had not been using the money I was giving them to pay the rent. And to top it off, Tiffany was stealing from the diner where we worked. The owner, knowing we lived together, figured I was in on it too and let me go. Five years of employment meant nothing to my boss. Not once in five years did I miss work or call in sick. All it took was for a wayward employee/roommate to sway his thoughts of me. Six months later, this is what my life has become. But no matter how bleak the future looks, I refuse to give up. I want so desperately to believe the words the older man at the library told me.

Sighing, I shake those thoughts away and peer down at my watch. I need to hurry. Unzipping my bag, I pull out the bar of soap I've been using sparingly for weeks. Turning the water on, I don't wait for it to heat before I begin washing my face, hands, and arms. Thankfully I was able to shower at the shelter the day before yesterday. I'm not always so lucky. Sometimes the beds fill up fast and I'm forced to sleep on the streets. Once I've finished washing, I pull on the black slacks and the light pink blouse. Both articles of clothing are way too big on my small 5-foot 2-inch frame, making me look like a child playing dress-up in her mother's clothes.

Shrugging, I do the best I can with what I have. Tucking the blouse into my pants, I use a safety pin to taper in the sides. Next, I dig in my bag for the pair of black two-inch heels I was fortunate enough to snag from the donation bin at the shelter. Any kind of footwear is usually snatched up within minutes.

Bracing my palm against the tiled wall of the bathroom, I slip the shoes on my feet. They are a size too small and have a few white scuff marks on the toes, but I make them work. Having sore feet is a minor price to pay if, by some miracle, I get the job. With my clothes and shoes on, I move onto my hair, and search through my bag for the one hair tie I have; only I can't find it. "Shit. Where is it?"

I look at the time again. "Dammit," I mutter just as I find the tie. Quickly, pulling my long strands back, still wet from the rain, I style my hair into a loose braid, draping it over my shoulder. Not wanting to put my dingy jacket back on, afraid to mess up my clean clothes, I shove it, along with my other belongings back into my backpack, then dash out of the bathroom.

By the time I jog the six blocks to the office building my interview is at, my feet are screaming, and I'm freezing. I swallow the lump in my throat when I look up at the towering structure before me. I take a deep breath. "You have nothing to lose, Denver. So, get your butt in there and get this over with."

Walking into the building, a blast of warm air washes over my face, and it feels incredible. I quickly spot the security station located in the middle of the lobby. "Can I help you, Miss?" one of the guards asks.

"I'm here for an interview with Mr. Hawk. My name is Denver Hollis."

The guard looks at his computer screen, tapping on the keyboard. "I see you here, Miss Hollis." He passes me a visitor's badge, and I clip it to my shirt. "Mr. Hawk's office is on the sixteenth floor. The elevators are over there to the right," he says, pointing. "Thank you," I say, nodding. As I go to step away, the guard stops me.

"I'm going to need to check your bag before you go up."

I freeze and turn back toward the man who is holding his hand out expectantly, then hand over my backpack. A wave of embarrassment washes over me as he unzips it and begins searching through my things. The guy eyes me but doesn't say a word at my old tattered clothes. Zipping the bag closed, the guard hands it back. Without another word, I make my way over to the elevator and ride it up to the sixteenth floor.

2

DENVER

Stepping off the elevator, I attempt to smooth out the wrinkles on my blouse as I make my way down a short hallway, and take in the grey interior and boring artwork that hangs on the walls. As I turn the corner, a woman is sitting behind the reception desk who looks to be in her late twenties to early thirties. She has black hair tied back at the base of her neck in a severe ponytail. A sign above her head reads HAWK LAW, CALLAN HAWK Attorney at Law.

When I reach her desk, she stops typing and looks at me with judgmental eyes. The corner of her lip tips up with what I am assuming is a look of disapproval. Tamping down my anxiety, I plaster a fake smile on my face. "Hello."

"Can I help you?" the receptionist asks as she lowers her head and goes back to her business as if she doesn't have the time nor the patience to deal with me.

"Yes. I have an interview with Mr. Hawk."

At my reply, her head darts up, her lips purse, and her eyes narrow. "Down the hall and to your left. Take a seat, and someone will be with you in a few minutes."

Doing as instructed, I walk down another hall until I see a second reception area. This one has a larger desk, and across from it are three chairs. I glance around the empty space finding no one around. Sighing, I take a seat in one of the chairs, fold my hands across my lap and wait. Soon, one-minute turns into ten and ten minutes turn into thirty. Looking down at my watch, I see my interview time was almost two hours ago.

Suddenly, the office door to the left of me bursts open, startling me. A moment later, I suck in a sharp breath at the sight of the tall, handsome man walking out. He is easily 6 feet 3 inches tall with broad shoulders, a chiseled jaw, perfectly styled dark brown hair, and striking eyes which match the color of his well tailored suit. A suit I'm sure costs more money than I've seen in the past two years.

With his phone to his ear and his expressionless face, it doesn't surprise me in the slightest when the gorgeous man doesn't spare me so much as a glance as he walks past me. It's not anything I'm not used to, though. Being overlooked is the story of my life.

Nevertheless, I continue to sit in the chair for another hour. Just as I am about to say forget it and leave, an older lady with a grey bob and a pair of reading glasses perched on her nose bustles past me with her arms loaded down with files, and abruptly stops when she notices me sitting there. The woman looks around, then back at me. "Are you waiting on someone, dear?"

I nod. "Yes. I am here for the personal assistant interview."

She looks down at her watch while trying not to drop the files. "That interview was over an hour and forty-five minutes ago. I'm afraid you've missed it."

I swallow and shake my head. "No. I was here five minutes early. The lady at the front," I point down the hall, "said to come in here and take a seat. She said someone would be with me in a few minutes."

"Lord, child. You've been waiting here all that time?"

"Yes." I take a deep breath. "I need this job. I'd still like the interview if it's at all possible. Please."

The woman sets the files down in the chair beside me and holds out her hand. "My name is Mrs. Marshall. You may call me Frances."

I shake her hand. "Hi Frances, I'm Denver Hollis."

"What a beautiful name, Denver. Why don't you come with me back to my office and we'll get you set up."

"For the interview?" I stand and go to help Frances with the files she is struggling with.

"Oh, honey, you already got the job. We need to get your paperwork squared away."

I stare blankly at her. "What do you mean I got the job? You didn't ask me any questions, and I thought I was supposed to meet with Mr. Hawk."

"Mr. Hawk has already left for court, so I am the one saying yes to you. Anyone who has the patience to sit here for almost two hours for a job they are not sure they will even get is the perfect person for the position. When it comes to Mr. Hawk, patience is something you will need a lot of if you are going to work here, dear."

"Let's just drop these off upfront with Kelly, and then we'll go talk in my office."

I'm assuming Kelly is the woman I met earlier when I arrived, and I'm proven correct when Frances stops in front of her desk and drops the files in front of her. I do the same with what I have in my hand. Kelly hangs up from her phone call and regards Frances with a sugary sweet smile. Nothing like how she greeted me when I first arrived. "How are you today, Frances?"

"I need you to take care of these files for me before you go to lunch, Kelly. Mr. Hawk will be expecting them back on his desk when he returns."

Kelly's eyes widen, and she sputters. "But, it's fifteen minutes until I break for lunch."

"Well, I guess you better get busy. I expect Mr. Hawk back within the hour."

Kelly huffs, but Frances ignores her. And just as she is about to walk away, she turns back to Kelly. "Oh. I almost forgot. Kelly, I'd like you to meet Mr. Hawk's new personal assistant, Denver Hollis."

"What!" Kelly screeches. "Mr. Hawk hasn't finished the interview process. He still has three more applicants, including myself. My application was the first one put in when his last assistant quit."

"Yes, well, Denver here has proven to be the most qualified thus far. I see no need to continue the search. I've also been permitted by Mr. Hawk himself to hire whoever I see fit, and I have decided Miss Hollis will do just perfectly."

With that, Frances turns on her heel and steps away from Kelly's desk. I wordlessly follow her. And just as we are about to turn the corner, Frances stops and looks back at Kelly, who is sending me a death glare. "One last thing, Kelly; next time you fail to announce one of Mr. Hawk's appointments, he will be notified."

Following Frances, we step inside her office. As she's closing the door, I say, "I take it Kelly wanted this job badly." I sit in the chair across from her desk.

"The last thing Mr. Hawk needs is an assistant looking to sink their claws into him. And that is exactly what Kelly wants to do."

"Oh," is all I can say.

Sifting through a stack of paperwork on her desk, Frances finds what she is looking for. "I have an employee packet you will need to take home and fill out. We need all the basics: Name, address, social security number. You know the drill." She hands the packet over, and I take it from her.

"How soon can you start, Denver?"

"I can start tomorrow."

"You don't have a current job which would require notice? When your interview was scheduled, there was no mention of current employment." She flips through the remaining papers sitting in front of her, finally producing my application form.

"I am currently not employed."

"Where did you last work? Do you have any experience being a personal assistant?" Frances asks.

My stomach drops. "No. I don't have any experience. My last job was as a waitress. But I can say in the five years of working at my last job, I never missed a day. I'm a hard worker, Frances, and will do whatever it takes."

Frances gives me a warm smile. "I have no doubt you will, sweetheart. I have a good feeling about you."

Her words instantly put me at ease, and I lose some of the tension in my shoulders. "Thank you. I promise to work hard."

As Frances goes about shuffling through more paperwork, my stomach rumbles with hunger, and my face flushes with embarrassment.

"Oh, my goodness. Will you look at the time? It seems we have both missed lunch. Would you like to continue this meeting in the deli downstairs?" Frances stands and looks at me. I have three dollars in loose change to my name. I have been saving that three dollars to use for washing my clothes at the laundromat.

"I'm not hungry, but I'd be happy to go down with you." My face heats as the lie rolls off my tongue. I can't help but notice the way Frances studies me.

Something flashes in her eyes before she speaks. "Don't be silly. Besides, lunch will be on the company's dime. It's the least we could do making you wait so long."

Nodding, I grab my bag that was sitting at my feet and stand. As embarrassed as I am, I'd be a fool not to accept the free meal. "Thank you, Frances. Lunch sounds nice." Once we make it downstairs, Frances leads me to the deli. "It must be nice to have such a place close by to grab something to eat. Especially with it being a cold and wet day like today."

"Despite his mood and reputation, Mr. Hawk is a good man. He had the deli put in a couple of years ago."

Frances steps to the counter and orders a chicken club sandwich, along with a salad. I order the same. After we are given our food, she leads us to a table in the back corner. That's when I ask, "Reputation?"

Frances cocks her head to the side. "Have you never heard of Callan Hawk?"

I shake my head. I'm not one to keep up with prominent people in business or the who's who of New York City. It's not like I have the resources anyway. My main focus in life is survival. And from the way the woman in front of me is looking at me, she seems shocked and pleased at the same time.

"The more I get to know you, Denver, the more I like you."

"Thanks...I think?"

Frances and I remain quiet for a few minutes as we eat our meals. I'm so hungry, I find it hard not to scarf down my food and make a pig of myself in front of her. Mindful of her observant eyes, I take small bites. Once I've eaten half of my sandwich, I wrap the remaining portion to save for later. Living on the streets and in the shelter, you learn to hoard what food you can because you never know where your next meal will come from. My thoughts quickly wander to the fact that I've been so hungry before that I've resorted to consuming food tossed into a trash bin on several occasions. Those points in my life have been some of my lowest moments. I sneak a glance toward Frances, who doesn't say a word when she sees me slip the wrapped food into my bag.

Needing a minute, I stand. "Will you excuse me while I use the restroom?"

"Of course, dear." Frances smiles, warmly.

I go to grab my bag when she stops me. "Why don't you leave your bag here. I'll watch it until you get back."

I don't usually let my backpack out of my sight since it holds everything I own. It's not much, but it's all I have. Living on the streets, you learn to guard what you have with your life. Studying her for a moment, I conclude I can trust Frances, and let loose of my bag. "Thanks. I'll be right back."

Finished with my business, I step out of the stall, then up to the sink and start washing my hands. I'm momentarily startled when I catch Kelly's ugly sneer in the mirror. "I don't know what you did to get that job, but I can tell you now, you won't last a week."

I lift a brow and shrug. I'm not one to entertain cattiness.

"I mean, just look at you." Kelly cackles as she tosses her towel in the trash bin, then leans her hip against the counter, her eyes traveling the length of my body. "Where did you get that outfit anyway; the bargain bin at the thrift store?" My stomach knots with humiliation.

"Mr. Hawk is a well-known member of the community. He needs someone with style and class representing him. He's going to take one look at you and see you are not the right person for the job. And when your ass gets canned, I'll be there to fill your position. Just as I should have in the first place." With those parting words, Kelly saunters out of the restroom with her five-inch red bottom heels clacking on the tiled floor. Everything Kelly said is true, but I'm not going to let it stop me from doing the best job I can, and pray that what she said about my new boss isn't true. Hopefully when Mr. Hawk finally gets a look at me, he doesn't send me packing.

By the time I make it back to the table, Frances has finished eating and pulled out a tablet. "Now that we have eaten, how about we get back to business?"

"Sounds good to me." I smile while putting my run-in with Kelly aside. She's not worth my time or energy.

"Will you be okay with coming in an hour early tomorrow morning? Say 7:00 am? That way, I can get you set up with Mr. Hawk's schedule and show you the computer system. I've been running things for Mr. Hawk since his last assistance quit. Be fore-warned, Mr. Hawk can be demanding, and your workload will seem hectic at first, but I will start you out slow. Once you get the hang of how things work, I'll start giving you more responsibilities. How does that sound?"

"Sounds perfect."

"Just the words I wanted to hear."

I smile. In the short amount of time I have spent with Frances, she has shown to be a lovely and patient woman. She reminds me of how I imagined a grandmother would act.

"Okay, Denver. Let's talk pay. As a new employee, you'll be placed on a mandatory ninety-day probationary period. Starting salary is fifty thousand a year. If you make it past the ninety days, your salary will increase to seventy-five thousand a year. This will include a yearly bonus, two weeks of sick leave, and two weeks of vacation. If you make it past a year, we will sit down with Mr. Hawk and renegotiate these terms. Do you agree with my current offer?"

I nearly fall out of my chair at the mention of fifty thousand dollars. I wasn't even making half of that at the diner. It takes me a second to realize Frances is staring at me expectantly because I have yet to answer her question. "Yes!" I blurt.

An hour later, after Frances and I finish ironing out the details of my employment, I leave the office and make the ten block trek to the shelter. By the time I get there, a line has already started to form. The housing only has a limited number of beds available every night. If you want to be guaranteed a spot, you need to be in line by at least 5:00 pm. I was relieved when Frances said I was off every day at 4:00 pm. That leaves an hour to walk from work to the shelter. I also figured that after a month of working, I would have enough saved to get into a small apartment of my own. Getting in line with the others, I wait. Only thirty more days. I can do it.

Later in the night, I lay awake on the cot, finding myself too anxious to sleep. I'm also hungry. Remembering the half-eaten sandwich in my bag, I sit up in bed and grab my backpack from the floor. Opening it, I gasp. Covering my mouth with the palm of my hand, I quickly look around making sure I haven't disturbed the person sleeping beside me, then look back in my bag. Not only is my leftover lunch there, but also a white paper bag with two blueberry muffins, a bag of chips and two bottles of water.

It must have been Frances.

In the cot next to me, I hear a rustling sound, and I glance at the pregnant woman sleeping there. Even in sleep, she has the weight of the world written all over her face. Looking down at the food in my bag, then back at the woman, I take one of the muffins, my leftover chicken sandwich, a bottle of water, and place the items in a bag, then quietly set the bag beside her pillow.

3

DENVER

Walking to my first day of work the next morning, I curse New York's weather. It's mid-November and currently thirty degrees. It could be worse. Thank God it's not snowing. The blouse I'm presently wearing does nothing to keep me warm.

Hopefully, mother nature will hold off until I get my first check and I can buy a winter coat. I hate to spend any of my money on extras because my main goal is to get out of the shelter and into an apartment, but the coat is something I can't do without much longer.

Rounding the corner, the frigid wind whips at my hair and causes my nose to run. Hugging myself to keep warm, I approach the entrance to my new workplace. As I go to step up to the door, a sleek black sedan pulls up to the curb, and a man exits the driver seat and makes his way to the back-passenger door. When the door opens, out steps the same guy I saw yesterday: dark hair, chiseled jawline, and a crisp expensive navy suit. Stopping, I stare. The man is genuinely breathtaking. Everything about him exudes power, money, sex. Once again, his phone is plastered to his ear as he walks past me. I'm mesmerized as I watch the reaction of those around him. Women blatantly ogle him, and men greet him with a nod. It's not until after he disappears into the building, I regain my senses and make my way inside.

The security guard from yesterday recognizes me instantly. "Miss Hollis," he greets.

I smile and give him a little wave as I continue on my way to the elevators. I half expected Kelly to be the first face I see when stepping out of the elevator, but she and her disapproving glare are nowhere in sight. Frankly, I can do without seeing her at all.

When I make my way down the hall, Frances is already seated at my desk, waiting for me. "Good morning, Denver. How are you this morning?"

"Good morning, Frances. I'm okay."

Frances waves me over. "Come sit, so we can get started." She points to the filing cabinet to our right. "You can store your bag here if you like."

Nodding, I tuck my bag into the cabinet, then grab the extra seat nearby and sit next to her at the computer. Over the next hour, she shows me the system and how to navigate Mr. Hawk's calendar. "This Post-It has the names of the people who you are to let through to Mr. Hawk immediately. All the others you take a message—no matter how persistent they are. Got it?"

"Yes. Always take a message aside from those here." I point to the Post-It.

Frances stands and pushes her chair aside. "Well, I'm going to leave you to it. I think you'll do just fine, dear. Remember I'm down the hall in my office if you need anything. Or press extension 202 on your phone. Don't hesitate with any questions you may have."

"Um...will I be meeting Mr. Hawk today?"

"You will." She smiles. "Mr. Hawk comes in early every day. He's already in his office." Frances points to the door directly across from my desk.

Over the next few hours, I become immersed in my new role.

Frances was right; Mr. Hawk is a busy man. Luckily, the constant influx of calls had gone a long way in helping me learn the ropes. Or so I thought. It was nearing noon when the door across from my desk burst open. My new boss emerges, and he does not look happy. I freeze as Mr. Hawk appraises me with his piercing green eyes. The kind of green that reminds me of spring-time in the park. And holy mother of God, he's even more striking up close. Lost in his eyes, I didn't realize how close he'd gotten. Suddenly, Mr. Hawk looms over my desk. I have no choice but to tilt my head back. His face is dark, and his stare holds me captive. My heart rate picks up. I keep waiting for him to say something— only he doesn't. "Hi," I say, barely a whisper. Mr. Hawk still doesn't say a word as his nostrils flare, so I continue, "My name is Denver, Denver Hollis. I'm your new assistant." I nervously extend my hand to him.

Mr. Hawk ignores my hand as his intense green eyes continue to hold my blue one's captive, causing me to squirm in my chair. *What is he waiting for?* Oh, crap! I must have screwed something up. That's why he's looking at me like that. "I'm sorry," I squeak, thinking I must have done something wrong. I try desperately to keep my bottom lip from quivering and hold back the tears that threaten to spill. I can't lose this job.

Mr. Hawk flexes his fists down to his sides before he, without a word, turns on his heel and storms back into his office, slamming the door.

What the hell just happened? My shaking hand drops to the desktop, and I finally feel like I can breathe again.

A few minutes later, Frances walks up to my desk and informs me I can go to lunch. Needing to calm down, I waste no time grab-bing my bag from the filing cabinet and making my way toward the elevator while avoiding Kelly's daggers along the way. Approaching the elevator, I glance over my shoulder to see Mr.

Hawk heading in my direction. Making a hasty decision, I duck into the stairwell off to my right. With my hand clutching my chest, I drop my butt down onto the step and try to calm my racing heart. "Get it together, Denver." I've never had a man affect me this way.

I end up spending my entire lunch break sitting in the stairwell while eating my blueberry muffin. When I return to my desk, there is no sign of Mr. Hawk, and I don't see him for the rest of the day.

"So, how was your first day?" Frances asks as we walk out of the office together.

"Good. I think I'm getting the hang of things."

"That's wonderful. I knew you would. Did Mr. Hawk give you a hard time? I promise he's not all that bad once you get to know him."

I fiddle with the strap to my backpack as we step out onto the sidewalk. I shiver the instant the cold hits my skin. "Mr. Hawk was fine." A gust of wind picks up, and I wrap my arms around my waist.

"Child, where on earth is your coat? You're going to freeze to death out here," Frances hedges, her voice full of concern.

"Oh, I'll be okay. Stupid me forgot it this morning."

"Do you want me to give you a ride, Denver? I hate to think of you walking in the cold."

I wave her gesture off. "I can catch a cab. It's no problem."

"Well, if you're sure." Frances gives me a worried look.

"I'm sure." I start to walk away. "I'll see you in the morning, Frances."

"Bye, Denver. See you tomorrow."

Later that night, after taking a shower at the shelter, I sit on the edge of my cot and inspect my feet. Blisters cover almost every toe and the sores on my heels have started to bleed. Lucy, one of the shelter workers, sits down next to me and passes me a bottle of peroxide along with some band-aids.

"Here you go. You don't want your feet to get infected."

"Thanks." I give her a small smile.

"What size do you wear?" Lucy asks.

"Seven."

"What have you been wearing?"

I point to the shoes on the floor. "Those are a six."

Lucy winces. "I'll keep an eye out for something in your size."

"Thanks, Lucy. I appreciate it." I smile.

Sometime in the middle of the night, I wake to find a man crouched down next to my cot with his hand on my backpack.

"What the hell do you think you're doing?"

The man startles but quickly recovers. "I wasn't doin' nothin'."

The alcohol on his breath washes over my face, and I nearly gag. "Get away from me." I snatch my bag away from him and hug it to my chest. Nothing my ass. I know what he was doing. He was looking to swipe my bag. When I think about it, it's not like I have the right to be angry at the man. I'm a thief myself. That alone makes me just like the drunk man currently staggering away from me as he makes his way back to the opposite side of the shelter.

I continue to lay there for the next few hours while sleep evades me. The time allows me to reflect on what I want out of life and how I plan to get where I want to be. So much has happened in recent months. Up until a couple of days ago, my future was looking bleak. I started to doubt if there was a light at the end of the tunnel. My motto has always been to take one day at a time. Try not to worry about tomorrow. Focusing on the here and now, remains my main concern. I know better than anyone how life can change in the blink of an eye. All it takes is one bad decision or, in my case trusting the wrong person to have a somewhat comfortable life turned upside down. My life before was far from perfect, but I had a roof over my head, a steady paycheck and food in my stomach. Through all of this, I still refuse to give up hope. Hope is what keeps me going. Despite the shitty hand I was dealt, I believe my hardships are happening for a reason. God never gives us more than we can handle, or that's what I remind myself of daily. I haven't given up hope that God has a plan for me. Not yet anyway.

Closing my eyes, I take a deep breath. My stomach decides at that moment to let out a loud growl. I still have that bag of chips, but I'm desperately trying to hold on to them. When my tummy growls for a second time, followed by a cramp, I give in to my hunger and dig the potato chips out of my bag.

As I open the small bag, I start thinking about where my next meal will be coming from. At work, I noticed a small pack of crackers on the counter in the employee's lounge next to the coffee maker. Maybe tomorrow I can pocket a few and hope nobody will notice or even care if they are missing.

On that thought, I savor the salty flavor as it explodes across my tongue. I've mostly been surviving on peanut butter when I can save up enough money to buy it. It's either that or Ramen noodles. A couple of times a week, the shelter feeds us, but like with the clothing donations, it's a first come first serve basis. There are times I have stood in line for two hours only to get turned away because they ran out of food. And bless her, on the days Lucy volunteers, she makes it a point to set aside a plate for me. That's not something she is allowed to do but she does anyway. I suspect she has a soft spot for me because we are the same age. Lucy comes from a great family and is a college student. What Lucy does for the other people who frequent the shelter and me is not out of pity, but out of compassion. The world needs more people like her.

4

DENVER

I walk into work fifteen minutes early with a bit of trepidation swarming in my gut. The office is quiet as I stroll past Kelly's desk finding it empty once again. When I reach my desk, murmured voices coming from Mr. Hawk's office catch my attention. I'm usually not a nosy person, but when I hear Mr. Hawk mention my name, my ears perk up. Setting my bag down on my desk, I look around to see if anyone is watching before I make my way over to his office door, which is slightly ajar. The next voice to speak is one I recognize; Frances.

"I don't see the problem, Callan. You needed an assistant, so I hired one."

"The problem is you didn't run it by me," he barks.

Oh, God. He's going to tell Frances to fire me.

"Seeing as you fired the last two assistants you had and I have been carrying double the workload for weeks now, I made the call to hire her. Did you or did you not say it was up to me? I believe your exact words were, 'just find someone competent enough to answer the phone.'"

I can't see Mr. Hawk, but I imagine him grinding his teeth right now. "Is she even old enough to be working here? She looks like she's still in fucking high school," he continues.

"Denver is twenty-three according to her ID, Callan. Also, watch your language." Frances's voice takes on a tone I have yet to hear from her before. "Besides," Frances continues, " the last two assistants you hired were nitwits. They didn't know their asses from their elbows. Hell, Callan, the last girl interrupted you while you were on a conference call because she couldn't find the power button on the computer."

"That's beside the point, Frances. I don't think Miss Hollis is the right fit for the job."

Frances and Mr. Hawk are silent for a moment before I hear the words I knew were coming.

"I want you to find me someone else."

"I will..."

Frances' words are cut short at the sound of Kelly calling out my name.

"Denver. What are you doing?"

I whip around to see Kelly standing behind me with her hand on her hip and a wicked gleam in her eye.

My face heats, and my heart pounds in my chest. "I was just going to see if Mr. Hawk wanted some coffee," I say as m

y voice shakes.

Just as Kelly goes to open her mouth again, I feel a looming presence directly behind me. I don't have to look to know who it is. Not only do I smell his woodsy cologne, but I can feel his heat against my backside. When Frances steps out of Mr. Hawk's office, I turn around.

"Good morning, Denver. Mr. Hawk already has his coffee. So, why don't you come with me and we'll get us a cup." Frances looks down at her watch. "We still have ten minutes to spare."

I don't think twice to follow Frances as she sidesteps Mr. Hawk. When I chance a glance over my shoulder, I see him still rooted in place with his heated gaze fixed on me. I also notice how Kelly stands next to him for several seconds, waiting for him to acknowledge her. With a huff, she gives up and goes on her way.

A few minutes later, Frances and I are fixing ourselves a cup of coffee in silence. As I am stirring in the cream and sugar, I feel I need to apologize. "I'm sorry for eavesdropping on yours and Mr. Hawk's conversation. It wasn't my intent. I arrived a little early, and when I heard my name..."

Frances waves her hand at me as she takes a sip from her cup. "No need to apologize, dear."

"Am I losing my job?" I ask.

Frances frowns. "Of course not. Don't you worry about Mr. Hawk. I can handle him. He knows I want you here and won't go over my head to fire you."

"You seem very comfortable with Mr. Hawk. How long have you worked for him?"

"Oh, I've known Callan since he was sixteen. He's very close to my husband. He's kind of like a son to us. I have been working here alongside him for close to seven years now. Ever since he opened this law firm."

Well, that explains why Frances has no qualms reprimanding Mr. Hawk on his cursing. I'm also curious as to how she came to know Mr. Hawk as a teen, but I don't ask.

The remainder of the morning passes quickly due to Frances adding more duties to my workload, which I found to be a bit overwhelming. At one point, I felt terrible for having to repeat questions, but Frances was patient with me. I nearly fell out of my chair when I saw how much Mr. Hawk charges for a simple consultation. Six hundred dollars for an hour of his time. He must be one hell of a divorce attorney because the man I talked to yesterday didn't hesitate to agree to the charges when he booked his appointment with my new boss over the phone. Being a bit curious, I took a quick peek at some other files, and found he takes on more pro bono cases than anything else.

Biting my lip, I let my curiosity get the better of me. Opening a second browser on the computer, I google the name, Callan Hawk. "Holy shit." The words tumble from my mouth. The first page that pops up is the most recent article in a tabloid magazine. Renowned attorney Callan Hawk slams the CEO of Loughtny Manufacturing, Richard Loughtny III in court. The Judge awards Mr. Loughtny's estranged wife 7.6 million dollars in money and assets. The second article I pull up is from five years ago.

Callan Hawk, age 31, son of the late Thomas Rawley, is set to inherit his father's multibillion dollar empire.

The article was five years ago. That would make Mr. Hawk thirty-six. Next, I pull up the image selection in Google to reveal photo after photo of Callan Hawk with numerous women on his arm. All socialites, actresses, and models. He doesn't appear to be photographed with the same woman more than once or twice, except one. The one I'm looking at now is of a model that he is pictured with the most. She has sleek black hair and is wearing a lavish white gown while clutching Mr. Hawk's arm at some gala, which doesn't surprise me. A man like Callan Hawk can get any woman he wants.

Not wanting to get caught Googling my boss on company time, I quickly close the browser and get back to work.

Thirty minutes later, I've just finished adding a new appointment to his schedule for next week when the phone on my desk rings. "Mr. Hawk's office, how may I help you?"

"Well, hello, sweetheart. To whom am I speaking?" the caller on the other end of the line drawls.

"Denver Hollis. I'm Mr. Hawk's assistant."

"Denver. What a pretty name. I bet your face is just as pretty as your name, Denver."

I blush, feeling my ears heat from his compliment. The guy sounds sweet. He also sounds like a hopeless flirt.

"Tell me, sweetheart, is Mr. Hawk in?"

"May I ask who's calling?"

"You can ask me anything." I hear the smile in his voice. "Tell him Spencer Knight is on the phone."

I recognize his name immediately. Spencer Knight is one of two names on the Post-It Frances gave me. "Hold one moment, Mr. Knight."

"Sure, thing, sweetheart."

I place Mr. Knight on hold and press Mr. Hawk's extension.

He picks up on the first ring and his clipped voice fills my ear. "What?"

I flinch at his tone. "I have a Mr. Knight on the phone for you."

"Put him through," he says before the line goes dead.

Asshole.

A few minutes later, Mr. Hawk steps through his office door and straight up to my desk. When his looming shadow lingers above me, my fingers pause over the keyboard of the computer and I look up. I go to ask him if he needs me to do anything, but before I can speak, he cuts me off.

"What were you and Mr. Knight talking about on the phone?"

My brow scrunches. "Nothing, Mr. Hawk."

"Really? Then tell me, why is he on a first-name basis with you?"

"He asked me my name, Sir." I swallow. "I didn't want to be rude."

Mr. Hawk's nostrils flare. "In the future, Miss Hollis, I would appreciate you didn't flirt with the people who call this office."

Flirt? What is he talking about? "I wasn't..." I go to defend myself only to be dismissed.

Mr. Hawk turns on his heel and heads back to his office. He calls out once more before slamming the door. "I have a friend

stopping by for lunch. I want you to order my usual from TARAN-
TINO'S along with an order of Antipasto Salad with Bocconcini
and green olives with a side of Vinaigrette dressing." I grit my teeth
at his flippant attitude toward me. Flirting?

There is no way I was flirting with Mr. Knight. Did he tell Mr.
Hawk I was flirting with him?

Brushing the incident aside, I place a call to TARANTINO'S.
Mr. Hawk's usual food orders are another thing Frances wrote
down for me. She said he's a creature of habit and rarely asks for
anything outside of the list. After placing the order, I immerse
myself back in my work. It's the sound of heels clicking on the
tiled floor that have me looking up from my computer screen. The
woman headed in my direction looks like she walked straight off
the runway; tall and willowy, has a perfect olive complexion, and
her straight midnight black hair hangs just past her shoulders. I
continue to stare. The woman's makeup is flawless. The way she
glides across the room on her five-inch heels while wearing a
white slouchy sweater paired with black leather pants, a fur coat
draped over one arm, and her Louis Vuitton bag clutched in her
hand, would make anyone stop in their tracks and take notice.

The woman saunters past me without so much as a glance. As
she goes to open Mr. Hawk's office door, I stand from my chair and
fly around my desk to stop her. "I'm sorry, but you can't just go in
there."

The woman stops with her hand on the doorknob. Slowly she
turns and glares down at me. She must be at least 5 feet 11 inches,
towering over me as her face morphs into a sneer. I suddenly
recognize her as the woman I saw on my computer earlier when I
was googling Mr. Hawk.

"You must be new here."

"Yes." I straighten my back.

The door to Mr. Hawk's office opens, and the woman in front
of me wastes no time wrapping herself around my boss. For some

inexplicable reason, something ugly settles in my gut watching them, and I cast my eyes away.

"Come in, Joslyn," Mr. Hawk addresses the woman whose eyes are still on me. Only this time, her sneer has transformed into a victorious smile. "Thanks, baby." She kisses him on his cheek. Through the whole interaction, Mr. Hawk keeps his focus on me and not the woman in his arms.

"Bring our lunch in as soon as it arrives," he orders, and I nod, keeping my eyes cast down at my feet. Just keep your head down, Denver. You can't afford to lose this job. Dealing with people like Callan Hawk and Joslyn is a small price to pay at the end of the day. Stay focused on your future—a place to live and food in your stomach every night.

When the food is delivered, I quickly make my way to his office. Knocking, I wait for him to answer.

"Come in."

"I have your lunch, Mr. Hawk." Stepping into his office, I find Joslyn sitting on top of his desk beside his chair, her legs crossed.

"Set it up over there." He jerks his chin toward the sofa and table on the opposite side of the room near the large window that overlooks the city.

Doing as I am told, I place the bag down on the table and begin pulling food containers out. The smell of grilled chicken and roasted potatoes fills my senses, causing my mouth to water and my empty stomach to rumble. I'm so hungry I'm on the brink of tears.

"God, Callan. Where did you find that one? The bargain bin down at the thrift store?" Joslyn does little to keep her voice down as she blatantly takes a dig at me. I pause what I'm doing and look down at the same pink blouse I wore the day before yesterday, the black dress slacks I have been wearing for three days straight and the too small, scuffed shoes on my feet currently screaming in pain.

Refusing to show weakness in front of my boss and his girl-friend, I ignore the jab and finish setting up their lunch. When I'm done, I exit his office without a word. Noting it is time for my lunch break, I stop by my desk, set the incoming calls to the answering service, and as fast as my feet will carry me, make my way to the stairwell at the end of the hall. I climb down one flight and fall to my butt on the same step I sat on the day before and allow the first tear to fall. I don't know why I'm letting Joslyn's words get to me. It's not as though I've never been judged and put down before. It's happened more times than I can count. The nagging feeling in the pit of my stomach makes me think it has everything to do with my new boss, and the way he just sat in his chair as his female friend berated me. I'll never be able to under-stand women like her. Women who tear down others to feel good about themselves; to make themselves feel as if they have some power over the other person. I could never treat another human being that way. There is no satisfaction in another person's pain.

Taking a deep breath, I close my eyes, wrap my arms around my middle, and lean my face against the cold concrete wall. I'm hungry. One of the coping mechanisms I use to ignore the pains from lack of food is to count. I have a thirty-minute lunch break. That's one thousand eight hundred seconds. So, starting at one thousand eight hundred, I count backward to myself.

I stop counting when I feel a presence behind me. Turning my head, I glance over my shoulder, to see Mr. Hawk standing in the stairwell several steps above me. As I wipe the tears from my face, I notice how his large hands grip the metal handrail with such force his knuckles begin to turn white. This time I don't shy away from looking at him. There's no point. He's witnessed my little breakdown and there is no denying I've been crying. I'm the first to speak. "I'm on my lunch break, Mr. Hawk, but if you need me, I can cut it short." I'm proud of how strong my voice sounds at the moment.

"No. That won't be necessary," he grinds out before walking away, which seems to be a trend with him.

By the time my workday is over, I am emotionally drained and slightly embarrassed for the events that transpired today. Not only was I treated like a pile of dog crap, but my boss caught me all up in my feelings about it. Not that I have anything to be ashamed of. We all have breaking points. I just rather no one would have witnessed my moment of weakness.

"You finished for the day, Denver?" Frances asks as she walks up to my desk with her coat, purse, and briefcase in hand.

I smile. "Almost. I have this one last email to send off to Judge Harrell for Mr. Hawk, and I'll be done."

"Great. Do you have any plans for dinner? My husband and I would love to have you over."

God, the invitation for a free hot meal sounds like heaven, but I don't want to lose my chance at a bed tonight. It's either food or a place to sleep other than the street. Plastering on a fake smile, I answer, "That's sweet of you, Frances. But I'm meeting a friend later. Can I get a rain check?"

"Of course, dear. If there isn't anything you need help with, I'll see you tomorrow."

"Nope. All good here. I'll see you tomorrow."

Once I have clicked send on the email, I power off the computer then grab my bag from the filing cabinet. As I make my way down the hall, I stop by the employee's lounge, spotting a pack of saltine crackers lying on the counter next to the refrigerator. I peer over my shoulder, finding no one around. A sense of guilt washes over me with what I am about to do, but I do it anyway. Swiftly I dash in, swipe the crackers off the counter, tuck them into my bag then quickly make my way to the elevator.

As I step out into the bustling city streets, the bitter cold cuts at my exposed flesh like a sharp razor blade. Trying to shield part of my body from the wind, I tuck my backpack close to my chest, hearing the cracker crinkle inside. I do what I have to in order to survive another day, but stealing something so simple still eats me up inside.

I walk briskly, weaving in and out of the crowds of people as I make my way to the shelter.

One day at a time.

5

DENVER

Finally, Friday!

When I arrive at work, I do so with a smile on my face. I survived my first week here, and that is a huge accomplishment. Sitting down in my chair, I fire up my computer and open my email to see my boss already has a laundry list of things for me to do this morning: have his dry cleaning sent out, call his housekeeper, and give her a list of items he needs picked up, place his lunch order, and set up a meeting with Janice, the records clerk for this afternoon.

"Am I going to get my coffee sometime today, Miss Hollis?" Mr. Hawk's voice rings out over the speaker on the desk phone, causing me to jump. He gets me every damn time he does that.

I press the button on the phone and reply. "Yes, Sir. I'm getting it now." Jumping from my seat, I shuffle down the hall to the breakroom, coming to a dead stop just outside the door when I hear my name spoken.

"I don't know how she has made it a week. I bet she doesn't make it another before Mr. Hawk fires her." I know that annoying voice. Kelly.

"Really?" Another woman's voice I don't recognize speaks.

"Frances has nothing but good things to say about her. She was telling Lucas the other day that Mr. Hawk was pleased with how she was doing."

I ran into Lucas two days ago. He's a paralegal here and is also the grandson of Roland, the older man from the library. Lucas was sweet when he introduced himself to me. I thanked him for both his and his grandfather's help getting me this job.

"Oh, please. I'm not buying that innocent girl act Denver is putting on. If you knew what I know about her...."

"What are you talking about, Kelly?" the other woman hedges. "Spill the dirt."

My nerves kick in, and my stomach starts to knot as Kelly continues. "I've been catching her stealing food." At Kelly's admission, my heart rate picks up and my body begins to shake.

"What! Stealing food?"

"Yep. Denver has been stealing food from the office. I've seen her do it. At the end of the day, when she thinks everyone is gone, she slithers in here like a snake and takes stuff."

The two are quiet for a second before the nameless woman speaks again. "I don't know, Kelly. Maybe you have it all wrong. It's only food. It's not like it's a big deal anyway."

"Not a big deal? She's probably stealing more than just food, Kara. Who knows what else her sticky fingers have gotten hold of? I'm going to be taking my concerns with Denver to Mr. Hawk. I'm sure he doesn't want a thief working for him."

Oh, God. I knew Kelly would be gunning for me. This is just the ammunition she needs to get me out the door. I have to get out of here.

With the whooshing sound of my heart pounding in my ears, I move on autopilot. When I reach my desk, my hands shake as I fumble with the drawer to the filing cabinet, where I snatch my bag up. Turning away from my desk, I come face to face with Mr.

Hawk—his brow furrowed. For a moment, I get lost in his mossy green orbs. I cock my head to the side to study him because, for some reason, his mouth is moving, but I don't hear his words. I only hear the rapid beat of my own heart. Then suddenly, I stumble backward. Tiny flashes of light begin flickering around me, and my vision blurs. The last thing I remember before everything goes black is the feel of Mr. Hawk's strong arms cradling my body.

I wake sometime later to the sound of Frances's voice. "Do you know what happened?"

I crack my eyes open to the sight of Mr. Hawk, pacing back and forth in front of me, becoming momentarily confused. Why am I in his office? And what the heck am I doing lying on his sofa?

I'm only confused for a moment before remembering Mr. Hawk was asking for coffee and overhearing Kelly talking to someone about me stealing food. Then Kelly said she was going to tell Mr. Hawk what I had done.

"I don't know what the hell happened," Mr. Hawk growls. "I called my doctor. He's on his way."

Doctor? Oh, hell, no. I let out a groan as I go to sit up. "I don't need to see a doctor."

Frances rushes to my side. "Denver. Good lord child. Are you okay?"

I don't get a chance to answer Frances because, like always, my boss cuts me off. "No, she's not okay. And you will be seeing a doctor."

Having enough of his bossy attitude, I shoot daggers at him. "I don't see how that is your decision."

"Seeing as you passed out and I had to catch you before you busted your head open on the floor, it most certainly makes it my decision," he snarls.

There is a knock on the door interrupting our standoff, and an older gentleman with a warm smile and wearing glasses strolls in.

I cut my eyes to Frances, who has yet to make another peep. I squint my eyes at the goofy look she's sporting as her eyes dart back and forth between my boss and me.

"Thank you for arriving so quickly, Dr. Morgan," Mr. Hawk greets the older man.

"It was no problem, Callan. Now, can you tell me what the emergency is?"

Mr. Hawk points to me. "My assistant, Miss Hollis, passed out about twenty minutes ago. She's been awake for five."

Dr. Morgan turns his attention to me. "Hello, young lady. If it's alright with you, I'd like to check you over."

I peer over Dr. Morgan's shoulder to my boss, who is giving me a look that says he dares me to say no. "Sure. But I'd rather not have an audience."

"I'm staying," Mr. Hawk grinds out.

Dr. Morgan peers at my boss over the rim of his wire glasses. "If my patient wants you to leave, I have to abide by her wishes. You may have called me here, Callan, but I still have to uphold doctor-patient confidentiality."

"That's no problem, dear. Callan and I will wait out in the hall." Frances gives Mr. Hawk a pointed look while trying to usher him out of the office. Finally, he relents and steps out of the room. I don't miss the way he grinds his jaw or the fact he was seconds away from breathing fire from his mouth. The man is confusing. One minute he acts as if he can't stand the fact that I am working here, and the next, he's worried about my wellbeing and demanding he be allowed to stay in the room while a doctor looks me over. I'm convinced Mr. Hawk has multiple personalities. I'm also confident I have the same disorder because one minute, I hate the man, and the next, I get butterflies in my belly from the way he looks at me.

Once Dr. Morgan finishes assessing me by listening to my heart and shining his penlight in my eyes, blinding me, he gives me a look and I already know what's coming. "When was the last time you ate, Miss Hollis?"

"Did you mean what you said about confidentiality?"

"Absolutely. Whatever is discussed in this room stays between the two of us," Dr. Morgan assures.

Too mentally and physically drained to lie and make excuses, I tell the truth. "Yesterday morning."

Dr. Morgan rears back. "Why have you not eaten anything in over twenty-four hours? No wonder you passed out. I have to warn you, Miss Hollis, you are doing serious damage to your body by denying it proper nutrition. Are you on one of these silly fad diets?"

I blow out a breath and squeeze my eyes shut. "Yeah. It's called the 'I'm homeless and have no money for food' diet, Dr. Morgan." Placing my elbows on my knees, I lean forward and rest my forehead in the palms of my hands.

"I see," Dr. Morgan says, his voice gentle. "Does Callan know of your current situation?"

"No!" I snap my head up. "Nobody knows, and I want to keep it that way."

"If Callan knew..." Dr. Morgan goes on to say.

I hold my hand up to stop him. "I don't want my boss to know I'm homeless. I don't need his or anyone else's pity. I can take care of myself. I'm also saving up to get myself an apartment. I'll only be in this predicament for a couple more weeks." I fold my arms. "I don't need anyone." By the look on my face and the tone in my voice, Dr. Morgan can sense the matter is closed. Slowly losing some of my defenses, I say, "Look, I'll try to do better about eating. I get my first check soon. I have a plan to start looking at apartments soon. I can assure you my situation is only temporary."

"Okay, Miss Hollis. For now, I am going to give you my number. I want you to call me day or night if needed." Dr. Morgan pulls a card from his pocket and scribbles his number on the back then hands it over. "I don't agree with the fact you won't say anything to Callan or even Frances, but I will respect it." He gives me a pointed look. "Your health comes before pride, Denver."

I take the offered card with a nod. I don't have any intention of ever telling Mr. Hawk anything.

Standing, I follow Dr. Morgan out of the office, where a worried Frances and my brooding boss are waiting. I ignore Mr. Hawk as he talks in hushed tones with Dr. Morgan. By the glare on his face, he is not pleased with the fact the doctor is not willing to divulge any of my information. Meanwhile, I take a seat back behind my desk.

"What are you doing, Denver?" Frances asks.

"I'm getting back to work," I shrug as though it was clear.

"I don't think that is a good idea. Perhaps you should go home and get some rest."

I give Frances a warm smile. She truly is the sweetest lady. "I'm fine, Frances. Really. I was in such a rush this morning I forgot to grab some breakfast. That and I have been feeling a little under the weather, and took some medicine on an empty stomach." I let the lie roll off my tongue. "I'll have some lunch in a little bit and be as good as new."

"The hell you will," a gruff voice barks over Frances's shoulder. "You'll eat now, and you'll eat in my office where I can keep an eye on you. The last thing I need is a passed-out employee." Mr. Hawk turns to Frances. "Tell Kelly she is to handle all of Miss Hollis's calls for the next hour." He then turns to me. "My office, Miss Hollis. Now." Mr. Hawk turns and storms off and I'm left stunned. I look to Frances for help. Only she doesn't offer anything except a huge grin.

"You don't want to keep him waiting when he's in a mood."

Sighing, I brace my palms on my desk and stand. "Is he always like this with his employees?"

Frances's grin turns into a full-on ear to ear smile. "Nope."

When I step inside Mr. Hawk's office, I stand at the door, unsure of what to do. This whole situation has thrown me off kilter. "Sit," he barks as he stands at the mini bar with his back to me. I watch as he fills a glass with ice then pours a small bottle of orange juice into it. Grabbing a bottle of water from the small refrigerator, along with the glass of juice, Mr. Hawk's legs eat up the distance between us. As he makes his way toward me, I can't help but take him in. Today he is wearing a grey suit with a white button-down. The red tie he had on earlier is now missing, and the top two buttons on his dress shirt are undone, exposing a smidgen of ink. I'm now suddenly curious about what is under his shirt and the extent of his tattoo.

"Denver," Mr. Hawk growls, catching my attention. The look on his face says he knows I was checking him out and I can feel my face flush. This is also the first time he has called me by my first name. I'd be lying if I said I didn't like the way it sounded on his lips.

I look up at his face and swallow. "What?"

He sets the glass and the bottle of water down on the table in front of me. "Drink."

This time I find myself not arguing. I pick up the glass of orange juice and place it to my lips, my boss watching my every move. I close my eyes and moan as the coolness slides down my throat. When was the last time I had orange juice? It tastes like heaven.

A knock at the door causes me to abandon my trance, looking up to find Mr. Hawk peering down at me, his eyes hooded. His green eyes draw me in, and without thinking, I run my tongue across my bottom lip. The grip my boss has on his bottle of water tightens, and the plastic makes a crackling sound under the pressure. The second knock on the door does the trick at snapping him out of his current state. The delivery guy stands in the doorway to the office, waiting for Mr. Hawk's orders. "You can set it down over here on the table," he tells him. Mr. Hawk pulls out his wallet and hands the delivery guy some cash. "Close the door on your way out, Dillon."

"Will do, Mr. Hawk. See you next time."

I find it endearing my boss is on a first-name basis with the guy who delivers his food. That thought causes me to smile.

"What's that look for?" he asks, taking a seat in the chair across from me and begins pulling the items from the bag.

"I think it's nice you know the name of the man who delivers your lunch," I shyly admit.

Mr. Hawk removes the lid to a plastic container and places it in front of me. In it is Thai chicken with a side of broccoli. It smells delicious. "Dillion has been bringing me my lunch at least three times a week for the past two years. I would be an asshole not to know his name, Miss Hollis."

I guess now we're back to Miss Hollis.

Together Mr. Hawk and I eat our meal in silence. I take my time to savor each bite, and the food is going a long way in making me feel better. As the minutes tick by, I become less nervous around my boss. He is abrupt with me, and kind of a bossy jerk, but has never been outright mean.

After I finish the last bite of chicken, I stand from the sofa and go about clearing the table. "Thank you for lunch. I already feel better." I toss the empty containers in the trash bin and turn to face

Mr. Hawk gives me a look as I leave his office. "I'll be at my desk."

6

DENVER

It's been three weeks since I started working at Hawk Law. Each day passes much the same. I'm bogged down with calls, emails, and appointment scheduling all day, and I like it. Staying busy makes the days go by much faster. Another plus is that I've saved the amount needed to put a deposit down on a place of my own. Tomorrow I'm meeting the apartment manager at noon to look at a studio apartment. It took me a week to find a place I could afford. It's not in a great neighborhood and the commute to work will be an hour, but it will be worth it to have my own place finally. The guy told me over the phone that the first month's rent and deposit are due on the spot. Rent is thirteen hundred a month and the deposit is five hundred. I breathed a sigh of relief when I opened my last check and it revealed I had made just enough over the last few weeks to cover the cost plus a couple hundred left over. I'm so giddy I can hardly contain my excitement. Tomorrow can't come soon enough.

"Miss Hollis." Mr. Hawk gives me a curt nod as he strolls past my desk with his briefcase in hand. "Did you get the Braxton file I asked for and email his lawyer's assistant?"

"Yes, Sir. I set it on your desk this morning. And I forwarded Granger's assistants' reply a few minutes ago."

Recently Mr. Hawk has been neck-deep into two new cases. So much so he called everyone into the office an hour early this morning. I don't mind, though. It's much better here rather than the shelter.

Standing, I round my desk. "I'll have your coffee for you in a minute. Also, Frances brought in some bagels from the bakery on the corner. Would you like one?"

With a jerk of his chin for confirmation, I set out for the break-room. I sigh when I spot Kelly fixing herself a cup of coffee. I don't say a word as I patiently wait for her to finish. Once she does, I grab a pod of Mr. Hawk's favorite brew from the cabinet, and pop it into the Keurig. The whole time I feel Kelly drilling holes into the back of my head. Continuing to ignore her, I grab a napkin and open the box sitting on the table to snag a bagel. Finally, having enough of Kelly's antics, I turn to face her. She has her hip propped against the counter as she casually sips from her mug.

"Is there something I can help you with, Kelly?"

"No. I'm just keeping an eye on you to make sure you don't steal anything."

My face heats. "I don't know what you're talking about. I'm not going to steal anything."

"That innocent little act you have going doesn't fool me, honey. I've seen it with my own eyes. You take food from here when you think nobody is looking."

"Kelly, I..."

"It's only a matter of time before Frances and Mr. Hawk see you for the lying little thief you are." Kelly takes two steps in my direction, coming face to face with me. "Your days here are numbered. And when you're gone, I'll be here to take your place beside Mr. Hawk, where I belong." Kelly shakes her head, giving me a look of pity. "I see the way you look at him. You're delusional to think he could ever be interested in a pitiful nobody like you. Someone who can't even bother to wash the coffee stain from the shirt she wore two days ago. Take a good long look in the mirror, Denver. You don't belong here, and Mr. Hawk would never look at you twice. You're his errand girl. His little mouse, who fetches his coffee and bagel."

With her cruel parting words, Kelly saunters out the door, leaving me feeling ashamed and embarrassed. If she's noticing the way I look at my boss, I wonder who else has. I look down at my shirt, and notice the stain I tried to wash out in the bathroom sink at the shelter the other day. Laundry day is Saturday. There was no way I could take my things to the laundromat after work and still have time to stand in line at the shelter for a bed.

"Good morning, Denver. How are you?" Lucas walks in with a grin on his face. I fix my features and shake off my encounter with Kelly.

"Hi, Lucas. I'm doing okay. How are you?" I grab a bagel for Mr. Hawk and one for myself, then finish my task fixing his coffee — black with two sugars.

"I can't complain. Not when I get to come to work and see your pretty face."

I blush at the compliment. Lucas has been friendly since I started working here, but he has never flirted. Or at least that's what I think he's doing. I could be wrong.

"So, how do you like working here, Denver? The boss treating you okay?"

I nod. "Yes. I like it here, and everyone has been nice." All aside from Kelly, but I don't tell him that. With Mr. Hawk's coffee and bagels in hand, I give Lucas a small smile as I head toward the door. "Speaking of the boss, I better get him his coffee."

"Say, Denver," Lucas stops me. "Would you like to go out sometime? There is a restaurant two blocks from here I think you'd like."

I look down at my feet to hide my red cheeks. Lucas is a handsome man with sandy blond hair and kind chocolate eyes. I'm tempted to say yes, but my current situation has me taking pause. I'm just about to turn him down when a familiar deep voice chimes in behind me. "She can't."

I peer over my shoulder to see Mr. Hawk standing there. His attention is laser-focused on Lucas.

"Oh. I didn't realize there was a no fraternization policy with the company, boss," Lucas states with a puzzled look.

"There's not," Mr. Hawk confirms with no further explanation.

I watch as several looks cross Lucas's face before it morphs into a smile. "I see."

I see? What does he see?

"Well, I better get to work. I'll see you around, Denver." Lucas nods toward me and then to our boss, leaving me confused.

Not knowing what just happened and with really nothing to say, I thrust the cup in my hand toward Mr. Hawk. "Here's your coffee."

He takes the cup from me, his fingertips brushing mine and my lips part. I can't seem to take my eyes off his striking features—his hard lines and chiseled jaw. When he still doesn't respond, which is nothing new, I swallow the lump in my throat and brush past him. "I'll get back to work."

After dropping off some files to Frances, I head back down the hall and notice Lucas standing by my desk. "Are you waiting for me?"

Lucas grins. "Some of us are going out after work for drinks. There is a bar down at the end of the block we all go to once a week. Do you want to join us?"

My mood deflates when I realize I have to turn his invitation down. I'm just about to decline Lucas's offer when Mr. Hawk's office door opens. His eyes dart between Lucas and myself standing within inches of each other, and his eyes narrow. I'm thinking he's going to be an asshole to Lucas again, but instead, he diverts his attention to me. "Grab your things, Miss Hollis. We have a meeting, make it quick."

My brow scrunches with confusion. "You don't have another meeting scheduled for today."

"I do now." His curt reply rubs me the wrong way as he heads for the elevator. "Now, Miss Hollis."

"Okay." Walking around my desk, I quickly grab a notebook, pen, and the new tablet Frances gave me this morning for taking notes and dash past Lucas in a hurry to catch up with my boss before the elevator door closes. "I'll catch you later, Lucas," I toss over my shoulder. Mr. Hawk's scowl turns into a look of irritation by the time I step beside him. As irritating as he can be, Mr. Hawk has an effect on me. My heart races and my palms become sweaty. I peek at him through my lashes, letting my eyes roam over his body. Lifting my chin, I catch his eyes on me as well, and my face heats. What is wrong with me? He is your boss, I silently chastise myself. Relief washes over me the moment the elevator doors slide open, and I feel like I can breathe again.

"Miss Hollis." He waits for me to exit, then follows close as we make our way through the first-floor lobby. When the two of us step outside onto the busy sidewalk, Mr. Hawk's driver is waiting for us beside a black car parked on the curb.

"Mr. Hawk, Miss Hollis." He dips his head. A cold breeze causes me to shiver, and Mr. Hawk takes notice. "Where the hell is your coat?"

"I forgot it," I lie.

Mr. Hawk grits his teeth. "Get in." He gestures toward the open car door.

Because I'm cold, I ignore his poor attitude, and slide into the back seat. Once Mr. Hawk climbs in, he addresses his driver. "Mitch, stop by the nearest department store. Miss. Hollis needs a coat."

"Yes, Sir."

"You don't have to buy me a coat. I'll be fine," I protest.

"It's not up for debate." At his last statement, he lifts his phone to his ear and turns his attention elsewhere, effectively dismissing me.

By the time we get to the restaurant, we're fifteen minutes late and I feel a tad guilty for being the cause. Nevertheless, the cream leather coat, with sherpa lining, is one of the warmest pieces of clothing I've had against my skin in a long time.

The hostess greets us the second we walk in, her eyes drinking in the sight of the man next to me. My lip curls at the way she eyes him, and an unfamiliar feeling of jealousy settles in my stomach.

"Good to see you again, Mr. Hawk. Your party is already here. Follow me, and I'll take you to your table."

The hostess sashays, adding an exaggerated sway to her hips as she leads us to our table. The older man already seated at our table stands. His eyes light up as he offers his hand. "Mr. Hawk, thank you for agreeing to meet with me."

Mr. Hawk doesn't offer any pleasantries in return. He nods and gestures for me to take a seat. "My apologies for being late, Mr. Dennis," Mr. Hawk tells the man. "This is my assistant, Miss Hollis," he introduces me.

Mr. Dennis, who has yet to take his seat, lingers at my side and places his hand in front of me. "Miss Hollis. It's a pleasure."

Not wanting to be rude, I tip my head back and look at the man. The vibe he gives causes me to recoil. Especially with the way his eyes linger on my breasts instead of my face. "Nice to meet you, too," I say, accepting his hand, and he holds on a little too long for my liking. Luckily, Mr. Hawk interrupts.

"I'd like to get on with the meeting."

Slipping my hand from Mr. Dennis's grasp, I maneuver my seat a few inches closer to my boss. I don't miss his look of approval at my action. Mr. Dennis chooses to take his place next to me instead of the one across the table. I look at Mr. Hawk. The set line of his jaw indicates he is not pleased with Mr. Dennis's behavior.

A few seconds later, the waiter arrives, takes our drink orders, and I take the opportunity to excuse myself. "I'm going to the ladies' room. I'll be right back," I whisper. Moments later, when I return to the table, Mr. Dennis has abandoned the seat next to mine and is now seated across the table. Both men are wearing tight expressions. Over the next hour, I listen to both men talk. Mr. Hawk grills Mr. Dennis about his wife, whom he is divorcing, along with asking him a multitude of personal questions. From what I've gathered, the guy sounds like a complete tool. He's painting himself as a model husband while making his wife out to be a cheating gold digger. I don't know Mr. Dennis or his soon to be ex wife, but something tells me that everything coming out of his mouth is a lie. I secretly hope my boss doesn't take his case.

A SHORT TIME LATER, I hear someone clearing their throat. "Excuse me." I look up from my computer hours later, to see a woman standing at my desk.

"Yes? Can I help you?"

"I have an appointment with Mr. Hawk. My name is Louise Dennis," she offers, her tone soft. I immediately recognize the woman's name. This is the wife of the man Mr. Hawk met with earlier.

"Yes, ma'am. If you'll come with me, I'll show you to his office." I knock on Mr. Hawk's door.

"Come in," he answers.

"Sir, Mrs. Dennis is here for her appointment."

Mr. Hawk stands from behind his desk and greets his client. "Mrs. Dennis, it's good to meet you. Please come in and have a seat."

I go to leave, but Mr. Hawk stops me. "Miss Hollis. I'd like you to stay and take notes."

That's a first. "Yes, Sir. Let me grab a notebook and pen from my desk." Notebook in hand, I take a seat in front of Mr. Hawk's desk, next to Mrs. Dennis, and I absorb the conversation between them.

"First off, I'll start by telling you I had a meeting with your husband."

Ms. Dennis' shoulders sag with a sense of defeat. "I figured he would get to you first. I assume you will be representing him during our divorce. I don't understand why I am here; why you reached out to me."

"After talking with your soon to be ex, I politely declined my services. I reached out to you because I'd like to represent you instead."

Mr. Hawk's admission stuns Mrs. Dennis. "I...I don't understand. My husband is a very successful man. He also has the means to afford a lawyer such as yourself. I, however, don't. My husband is leaving me with nothing. After twenty years of marriage, I am leaving the same way I came into it; penniless. He has literally supported me our entire marriage."

Mrs. Dennis's confession both shocks and angers me. How, after twenty years together, can a man toss his wife aside as if she were worth nothing?

"That is precisely the reason I am taking your case, Mrs. Dennis. I also will not be requiring payment for my services."

My heart warms, and my lips turn up into a smile. Over the past couple of weeks working here, I have begun to see a pattern with my boss. I see how he takes consultations with these rich and powerful men, charging them an extensive fee for his time, only to turn around and decline his services. He then turns around and contacts the spouses of these men. He takes on all those cases for free. I'm not entirely sure why he agrees to meet with the husbands, but I'm starting to admire the way Mr. Hawk does business.

"Miss Hollis, please set up another appointment for next week with Mrs. Dennis. And Mrs. Dennis, I'm going to email you a list of things I want you to bring the next time you come in. I'm going to put a call into Judge Franks and have the child support hearing pushed to tomorrow. It's my understanding your oldest son is away at college, but you have two other children at home? Has he helped support the children since the separation?"

Mrs. Dennis shakes her head. "My son's tuition is paid up for the semester, but my husband has not given me any support since we separated two months ago."

I watch as Mr. Hawk's face darkens. "That won't be an issue after tomorrow, Mrs. Dennis. You have my word."

The three of us stand. Mrs. Dennis looks as if the weight of the world is lifted off her shoulders.

"Miss Hollis. Call Judge Frank's office. Tell his secretary I need an early morning meeting tomorrow."

"Yes, Sir." I shuffle out of his office while Mr. Hawk walks Mrs. Dennis to the elevator. A few minutes later, he returns with Kelly trailing behind. In her hands are two white bags with the TARANTINO'S logo on the front. "You can set them down on the table in my office, Kelly." The delivery must have come while we were in the meeting with Mrs. Dennis.

Kelly saunters past me with her nose in the air doing what she is told. When she walks back out, she stops. "You know Mr. Hawk; Tarantino's is one of my favorite places to eat. They have the best Chicken Fettuccini in the city." She bats her eyelashes, and I duck my head to hide my eye roll.

Ignoring Kelly's blatant attempt at an invitation, Mr. Hawk addresses me. "Denver." My name is the only word he says, and I shiver at every use. It's the same every day since the day I passed out in the office. Lunch is delivered at noon. Mr. Hawk then orders me to eat with him in his office. I have managed to gain a few pounds in the past couple of weeks too. Acknowledging Kelly for the first time since she opened her mouth, Mr. Hawk turns to her. "Handle Miss Hollis's calls while she is at lunch."

Pursing her lips, Kelly strolls back to her desk. I'd be lying if I said it didn't enjoy her dismissal.

A small giggle escapes my lips as I take a seat on the sofa and pull our lunch from the bag. I also don't miss the grin that crosses Mr. Hawk's face. Our lunch is spent the same as the days before; in silence. That is, until a knock at the door, followed by Joslyn and all her beautiful glory float in. Stopping mid-stride, she accesses the scene in front of her with a look of heated anger, which is quickly replaced with a fake smile. "Baby," she whines and continues with a pout, "I wanted to surprise you and take you out to lunch but I see you've already eaten." Her eyes cut to me, narrowing to slits. "But don't worry, I can provide you with desert." Ignoring me, she saunters over to Callan and drops down in his lap, covering his mouth with hers.

My stomach drops. "I'll finish this at my desk," I say, my throat tight.

"Yeah. You do that," Joslyn sneers.

I don't say anything in return, and I refuse to look at my boss as I close his office door with a soft click. To top it off, Kelly is waiting for me when I exit.

"As I said, he'll never choose you over a woman like Joslyn."

"I'm not in competition with anyone, so I don't see how your statement is relevant," I fire back. "The only person here trying their damndest to get noticed like a cat in heat is you." Yeah, I went there. Because even though I am a person who tries like hell to avoid confrontation, I have my limits, and Kelly is testing them all. "Don't mistake my silence as weakness," I warn her.

"You better watch your back around me, Denver."

"You know what, Kelly. You sure do talk a lot for someone with nothing to say. Your threats don't scare me." I flick my hand and shoo her away.

"Whatever. You'll see," Kelly huffs as she's walking off.

With my appetite lost, I pick up the remainder of my lunch and decide to finish it elsewhere, and retreat to the break room for the duration of my lunchtime. No way am I sitting at my desk while Joslyn gives Callan his desert. The thought alone of his hands touching her, and not me, makes me green with envy. Where the hell did that come from? What is wrong with you Denver? Get yourself together. Walking down the hall, I square my shoulders. I have much more important things to worry about besides Callan Hawk, and what he's doing in his office at this very moment. Focus on yourself. I keep repeating those words in my head as I approach the breakroom. Lucas is sitting there eating his lunch when I walk in.

"Denver. We meet again." He throws another boyish grin.

"Mind if I sit with you?"

"A pretty lady never has to ask to sit by me."

Rolling my eyes, I take a seat. I'm starting to catch on to the way Lucas operates. I have a sneaky suspicion he's a player. "I bet you say that to all the girls, Lucas." My retort awards me a full-on smile, dimples, and all. Lucas is cute. In that boy next door kind of way.

"Only to you, Denver."

I laugh. "Liar. But I'll take the compliment anyway." I don't know what it is about Lucas, but he's comfortable to be around. His easy-going personality helps. His compliments make me blush. Not in the "I'm attracted to you" kind of way, though. It's not often someone like me receives a compliment. When Lucas does it, it feels foreign, Yet, makes me feel good.

"So, you and Mr. Hawk?"

I look up at him, confused. "What?"

"You don't have to play coy with me, Denver." Lucas nudges me with his elbow as he takes a bite of his sandwich.

"I don't know what you're talking about."

Lucas grins, a mouth full of food. "I'm sure you will soon enough, sweetheart."

"Whatever. You're talking crazy." I ball my napkin up and toss it at him.

"What's going on here?"

I peer over my shoulder to see Mr. Hawk has yet again busted mine and Lucas's conversation. "Nothing. We're eating lunch."

"I think lunchtime is over. Wouldn't you agree, Lucas?"

I answer for him. "Actually, we still have ten minutes."

Pushing his chair back, Lucas stands and begins cleaning his mess. "The boss is right. I should be getting back." Lucas tosses his trash in the garbage bin. When he walks past me, he places his hand on my shoulder and gives it a light squeeze. "I enjoyed this. Let's do it again sometime, sweetheart." With a wink, Lucas walks out, brushing past Mr. Hawk and I swear I hear him mumble "not fucking happening," under his breath.

Following suit, I stand. "In the future, if you require me to take a shorter break, can you please tell me in advance so we can avoid confrontation?"

"In the future, all of your lunches will be spent in my office, with me. Problem solved."

"Except on the days your girlfriend is here." I let the snarky reply roll off my tongue as I walk past him. Yeah, I went there.

7

DENVER

With the weekend finally here, I get ready for the day and even add a little pep in my step. I don't meet the guy about the apartment until noon, so I decide to go ahead and get my laundry out of the way. The good thing about weekends is I get to change back into my well-worn, secondhand jeans. Even though my shoes have a broad strip of duct tape covering a hole in the toe, they are more comfortable than my work shoes.

The laundromat I use is right around the corner from the shelter. When I arrive, I find it packed. Looking down at my watch, I see I have several hours until noon, so I don't fret. Besides, waiting inside for a machine to free up is better than waiting out in the cold. Luck was on my side today. There was a large clothing donation at the shelter this morning. I was able to snag two more shirts for work and they all needed washing before I can wear them. The articles are a little outdated, but beggars can't be choosy, right? Either way, I'm grateful. Every little bit helps, and I know I'm one step closer to getting my life back on track. Since there were no appropriate work shoes in the donation bin, I plan on buying myself a brand-new pair in a few more weeks. And, if I get that studio apartment today, I'll have just enough money left to purchase an airbed and do some grocery shopping.

Finally, after an hour and forty-five minutes, the couple who was hogging three washers and dryers finish. I only have enough clothes for one load, so I'll be in and out in no time. While waiting for my clothes to finish, I can't help but let my mind wander. The only thoughts that fill my head are of Callan. That man has taken up permanent residence inside my brain. It's stupid of me to be having the feelings I am, yet I'm completely powerless to stop it. I'm completely out of my element when it comes to him.

During high school, I focused on keeping passing grades and stressing about how long my current foster parents were going to put up with me before they decided they were finished with me. Seriously boys were not on my radar. Since I have been on my own, my days are spent trying to keep my head above water. At my old job at the diner, I was asked out frequently by customers. A few times, I said yes, but neither of those dates turned into anything.

Not that the guys weren't pleasant. There was just no spark. Callan Hawk is the first man to ignite something inside of me. It figures the first man to invoke anything is not only unavailable but out of my league. Hotshot billionaire Callan Hawk, a man known to only date supermodels being interested in a nobody like me? Can you imagine the two of us standing side by side? Him in his three thousand dollars suits and me in my second-hand jeans and shoes wrapped in tape. It's laughable really. I have no delusional fantasies of my boss and me. I sigh. "A girl can dream."

A couple hours later, the subway commute to where my potential new home is located took nearly an hour, and, now, I'm standing outside the building where the man I talked to told me to meet him. I look down at the piece of paper in my hand and back up at the numbers hanging on the brick wall next to the entrance, where three men are sitting drinking beer. They eye me with suspicion, and their attention makes me uncomfortable.

"Are you Denver?" a man stepping out of the door asks, and for a split second, I think about bolting. The guy in front of me is at least a foot taller than myself, is wearing a stained t-shirt, has greasy brown hair, balding at the top, and a cigarette hanging from his mouth. "Look, lady. It's colder than a witch's tit out here. Are you interested in the apartment or not?"

I go against my better instincts and answer the man. "I'm interested."

"Then come on in, and I'll show it to ya." The man disappears inside the building passing the three men as we make our way up the stairs. The first thing to hit me when I walk in is the smell of urine and stale cigarettes. "The studio is on the third floor. The elevator is out, so you have to take the stairs," the man tells me. "Name's Harold, by the way."

"Nice to meet you, Harold." I fake pleasantries.

"Here we are." Reaching what I assume is the studio apartment, Harold fishes a set of keys from his pocket and unlocks the door. He steps into the apartment first and I take a hesitant step behind him, leaving the door open and a few feet of space between us. I don't need to go any further because the place is small. To my left is a kitchenette, and to my right is an area large enough for a bed and possibly a tiny sofa. Shuffling forward a bit, I notice a door. I open it to reveal a bathroom. The appliances look to be older than me and the floor is an awful yellow linoleum. As drab as the place seems, all I can do is smile. "I'll take it."

"You got the money for the deposit and first month's rent on you? Because I'm not looking to waste my time. I got two other people interested in the place."

"I have the money. You said it was thirteen hundred a month with a five hundred deposit. Right?"

Harold smiles, showing his yellow stained teeth. "That's what I said."

Reaching into my bag, I pull out the exact amount of cash needed and hand it over. Harold stuffs the payment into his front pocket and passes me the key to the apartment in exchange. "The previous tenants are still in the process of gathering the rest of their things," he points to a pile of boxes beside the door. "And the gas won't be on until tomorrow. Will it be a problem for you to wait until tomorrow to move in? Wouldn't want you to freeze in here."

I shake my head. "No. Tomorrow is fine. It gives me time to get a few things for the place."

"Alright then, girly. You got yourself an apartment. Have a good day."

Harold goes to leave, and I stop him. "Wait. Do I need to sign a lease or anything?"

"Nope. You're all set."

I find it strange Harold doesn't require any written agreement, but this is my first time renting an apartment on my own. What do I know? Besides, by the looks of the building and the neighborhood, the people here don't look like they put much stock into formalities.

THE NEXT MORNING, after stopping at the store to buy a twin air mattress, I hop on the subway again with the biggest smile the whole hour commute to my apartment. When I arrive at my apartment building, no men are sitting on the stoop. Maybe because it's seven o'clock on a Sunday morning? Either way, I shrug and make my way inside and up the staircase. Using my key, I insert it into the lock, only to discover it doesn't fit. "What the hell?" Pulling the key out, I stick it back in and let out a nervous giggle. *No! This is not happening.*

I try knocking on the door in hopes the former tenants are still here and have a spare key. I bang on the door three times with no answer before trying the key once more. This time it breaks off in the lock. "Shit." There must be a mix-up. Harold must have given me the wrong key. I knock on the door again, this time a little harder. "Hello! Is anyone there?"

"Hey! Knock that pounding off, girl. You're going to wake up the whole damn building." A lady with a Latino accent chastises and I give her my attention. The woman is rail-thin with a weathered face and the kind of red hair that comes from a box.

"I'm sorry. But this is my apartment, and my key broke off in the lock. I was hoping the former renters were still here."

"No way is this your apartment, Chica. I'm the building manager, and I sure as hell, don't remember renting it to you."

"You're the manager?" My good mood suddenly vanishes.

"That's what I said. I should make you replace that lock you just broke, girl." The woman gripes with a cigarette hanging from her fingers.

"I...I rented this place from Harold. He's the one who answered the phone when I called about the online ad."

"Dios." The lady shakes her head. "That bastard Harold is the guy who lived in this apartment. I served him eviction papers a week ago. The son of a bitch scammed you. I'm going to bet you aren't the only person either."

"What!" I shout. "That can't be right. Please. I met him here yesterday. He showed me the apartment and took my money." I panic.

"I'm sorry, Chica. You got swindled. He and your money are long gone."

My body slumps against the wall as the contents of my

stomach threaten to make an appearance. The lady looks on with pity and sighs.

"Look. I can see you're in a bind. I can't get your money back, but I can still rent the apartment to you. Going to need eight hundred for the place." She pulls a drag from her cigarette, leaving red lipstick on the filter.

"Eight hundred!" I snap my head up. "I gave Harold eighteen hundred."

The woman nearly chokes on the cigarette she's smoking. "Eighteen fucking hundred. Shit, girl. Why the hell did you think a dump like this would go for that much?"

At this point, there is no stopping the tears from flowing past my cheeks. "I was thinking I was tired of living in the shelter and needed a home."

The lady places her hand on her hip. "I get it. But business is business, and I can't let you have the place without payment. I'm sorry." There is a hint of sympathy in the woman's eyes but not enough to waver on her deal.

I don't bother trying to negotiate. Pushing myself away from the wall, I shoulder past the woman. I have no one to blame but myself. I was the one naive enough to believe in a stranger, and in the end, I paid the price. I learned a valuable lesson today. Number one, you can't trust people and number two, karma is a bitch. This is the universe paying me back for being a thief myself.

I walk in a haze back to the subway station, my mind racing. I bump into a few people on the street who reward me with dirty looks. I don't have it in me to care or say excuse me. By the time I make it back to the subway, I realize my hands are empty. Shit. I left the air mattress back at the apartment, or dropped it somewhere. I contemplate going back for it because that's thirty bucks I can get back by returning it to the store, but quickly squash that idea. Someone would have swiped it by now.

Pulling my coat tighter around my body as I try to fend off the blistering cold, I step out of the subway onto the busy city streets. The hour-long ride has done little to calm my despair. I was supposed to be spending my first night in my new home. Instead, I am headed back to the shelter.

"Denver." Lucy rushes up to me the moment, and I step inside. "Are you okay? She looks me over. "What happened? I thought you were moving into your apartment today."

I wipe the tears from my face. "I was. But it turns out the guy I met with yesterday was not the apartment manager. He was just some guy who had been living there and was being kicked out. He placed a fake ad online. He took my money and is gone. I found out all this from the woman who is the actual manager."

"Oh, no. Denver, I'm so sorry. Does this woman know where you can find the man? Have you thought about going to the police? I can go with you if you want."

I shake my head. "Harold is long gone. I don't see the cops being able to do much. There is no telling how long it would take to track him down."

"It's still worth a try. Don't you think? Maybe the cops can find him and get some of your money back."

"No. I want to lay down and forget how stupid I was to believe my luck had turned around. I'm tired and I have work tomorrow."

"Alright." Lucy sighs in defeat. "Promise me you'll let me know if you change your mind about going to the cops."

Later that night, I toss and turn on the cot. The tears have stopped, but my eyes feel swollen and scratchy. I just hope I don't look like a mess for work in the morning. Taking a shuttered breath, I close my eyes. There is no sense in dwelling on what can't be changed. I lost almost all my money and what was to be a new start. But I still have a job. I'll keep working and keep saving. In a couple of weeks, I'll find another place to stay. Tomorrow is a new day.

8

DENVER

DENVER

"Miss Hollis!" Mr. Hawk yells from his office Monday afternoon. Not only did I get little to no sleep last night, but Mr. Hawk is especially grumpy today. So, you can imagine my ill mood, paired with his, was a cause for our constant head butting. Mine from the disastrous weekend, and being swindled out of my hard-earned money and his probably due to the fact he is working diligently on the Dennis case while preparing for court on another. We did get a bit of good news this morning. The judge granted Mrs. Dennis child support. He also ordered her soon to be ex-husband to pay two months back child support.

Getting out of my seat, I make my way to the open doorway of Mr. Hawk's office. "Sir?"

He looks up from a stack of papers on his desk, his green eyes narrow to slits. "Where are the medical reports on the Braxton case? I told you this morning to put them on my desk."

The Braxton case has been a tough one. It turns out, Mrs. Braxton had been a victim of domestic abuse at the hands of her husband through the course of their marriage. She was smart enough to keep medical records every time she visited the ER.

Those records will be vital when the case goes to court. I happened to take a peek at the files before placing them on Mr. Hawk's desk. My heart aches for what Mrs. Braxton has gone through. I hope Mr. Hawk buries her husband in court, although hell would be a better punishment.

"Yes, Sir. I put it on your desk first thing this morning."

He shuffles through the papers on his desk. "It's not here."

Sighing, I close my eyes and count to ten, trying not to say something I'll regret. I've gotten used to my boss being a prickly asshole, but he's seriously testing my limits today. Walking across his office, I stop in front of his desk, lean over, and pick up the report, which was right in front of him. When I cast my eyes up, I find Mr. Hawk's trained on my chest. The top button on my blouse got snagged on my coat this morning and popped off. I meant to find a safety pin to hold the top in place. And right now, my boss is getting a good look at my generous cleavage. My skin tingles, and my nipples harden to pebbles under his heated appraisal of my breasts. There is no denying the effect the man is having on my body. A growl vibrates within Mr. Hawk's chest when his eyes shift to the hard peaks showing through the material of my top.

"Here you go, " I say, my throat tight with lust.

When he finally rips his gaze away from my breasts and up to my face, I decide it is time to abort. Without another word, I turn on my heel and scurry back to my desk.

I spend the next thirty minutes analyzing what just happened between the two of us, and concluded Mr. Hawk is like any other man—momentarily boob drunk.

After delivering some paperwork to Frances down the hall, I'm met by a tall man standing at my desk with his back to me. "Can I help you?"

He turns, and I am met by the second most devastatingly handsome man I have ever seen. This guy stands well over six feet, has red hair, grey eyes, and a few days' worth of stubble on his face.

The man doesn't hide the way his eyes rake up and down my body. I don't know why he's bothering to look. I'm wearing one of the outfits I got from the donation bin at the shelter. Today my attire consists of a pair of brown slacks and a boxy cream color button-up blouse that is about two sizes too big aside from the boob area. I wasn't lying when I said the clothes were outdated. I'm wearing something straight from the eighties. My hair is pulled back in its usual braid and there isn't a stitch of makeup on my face. You would think by the panty-melting grin taking over the stranger's face, I was his dessert.

"You must be Denver?"

I recognize the voice instantly. This is the guy I spoke to my first week here, the one, my boss accused me of flirting with.

"I am. And you're Spencer Knight," I address him in a bored tone since he told Mr. Hawk I was flirting with him. I'm tempted to say go to hell, but don't want to risk losing my job.

"That I am, sweetheart."

"Mr. Hawk is in his office. You can go on in."

"How about I stay here and visit with you, sweet Denver?" Spencer says as he perches himself on the edge of my desk, making me glare up at him.

"With all due respect Mr. Knight, I have work to do. I also don't need my boss accusing me of flirting with you again."

Spencer goes to open his mouth again at the same moment Mr. Hawk makes an appearance. "Spencer!" he barks. "It would be in your best interest to step away from my assistant's desk," he warns, emphasizing the word "my" and causing my skin to tingle. It's clear these two men are friends rather than business acquaintances. It's also obvious Spencer is getting a kick out of pushing Mr. Hawk's buttons.

"Hey, Callan. I just thought I would get to know Denver better." Spencer stands and strolls toward his friend. "I have to say, Callan. I can see why your nuts are all tied up over the lovely Miss Hollis."

"Fuck off, Spenc," is the last thing that comes from Mr. Hawk's mouth before the two men disappear inside his office and I'm left wondering what Spencer meant by his comment to my boss.

The rest of the workday goes by without incident. Spencer was here about an hour, and as he left, tossed me a wink over his shoulder. I found I couldn't stay mad at the man, and waved. He's a lot like Lucas in the way he's a hopeless flirt.

It's four o'clock, so I begin shutting down my computer just as Frances strolls down the hall from her office with Kelly trailing behind. "Hi, Frances."

"Hello, dear. You knocking off?"

"Yep. You on your way out too?"

"I am. You want to walk down with me?"

"Yeah. Let me grab my coat, and I'll go with you." I smile.

"I'm going to need you to stay late, Miss Hollis," Mr. Hawk's gruff voice rings over my shoulder and I turn to face him.

"What?"

"Mrs. Dennis was unable to take off work to make her two o'clock appointment. I told her she could come in at five."

This was not news to me. I had taken Mrs. Dennis's call this morning, and Mr. Hawk agreed to let her come in after hours, although there was no talk of me having to be here too.

"You didn't mention earlier I was required to stay past four."

"I'm telling you now, Miss Hollis."

"I...I can't stay, Mr. Hawk."

"Why the hell not? Your job is to assist me. Therefore, you work when I tell you."

What am I supposed to say? I need to leave by four, so I can get a bed at the shelter before they are all taken?

Shoot, Denver.

Think.

Kelly perks up. "I can stay with you, Mr. Hawk."

Frances must sense my distress and tries to help. "There you go, Callan. Kelly has volunteered. That was nice of you to step in for Denver."

Kelly didn't offer as a favor to me. She suggested that because she's desperate for Mr. Hawk's attention.

"No. Kelly, you and Frances may go. Miss Hollis will stay and do her job," Mr. Hawk states, making his decision final.

Having moved the meeting with Mrs. Dennis to the conference room, so we had more space to go over all the documents for her upcoming court case, I sit in my chair, my leg bouncing with nervousness as I continually eye the clock on the wall. Mr. Hawk shoots me a look, but I ignore him. I don't understand why he pushed to have me here. Not once has he asked me to stay late. And now because he's decided to be a jerk, I'm most likely spending the night on the street. It's a quarter to seven and there is no hope of me getting a bed at the shelter.

On top of that, it started snowing an hour ago. The snow always draws in more people looking for a warm place to shelter from the dropping temperatures. I've braved sleeping outside on many occasions in the last six months, but never in this kind of weather.

"Mrs. Dennis." My boss stands. "I think we have all we need for court next week."

"You think what we have will be enough?"

"I know we do. I promise your husband won't be able to squeak by without having to pay."

Mrs. Dennis shakes Mr. Hawk's hand and offers me the same.

I accept while offering a polite smile.

"Miss Hollis. Gather everything here and put it on my desk while I walk Mrs. Dennis out."

Nodding, I go about clearing the table as quickly as I can and take it to his office. By the time Mr. Hawk returns, I have completed the only task he asked of me this evening. I'm in hysterics and pissed as hell as I go to gather my things to leave. "I'll walk you out."

"No," I snap, tugging my coat on, my hands shaking.

"Is there a problem, Miss Hollis?"

"Yes. The problem is you making me stay late for nothing. There was no point in me being here, Mr. Hawk," I say through clenched teeth. "And without notice." At this point, I can't hold back the choking sound that comes out at the end of my last statement.

"What's the matter, Miss Hollis? Did I make you miss a date with that prick Lucas or something?" The question falls out of his mouth with venom. I don't bother wasting my breath on a reply, and walk away.

When I exit the building, Mr. Hawk is right behind me. In front of us parked on the curb is his car with the driver waiting at the back door. "Come on, Denver. I'll take you home."

"No. I don't need anything from you."

"Will you stop being pissy with me long enough to accept a damn ride?" I don't turn around, and I don't accept his invitation.

"Denver!" Callan calls out at my retreating back. "Get back here and get in the fucking car!"

I keep going until I round the corner at the end of the block. Only then do I allow the tears to fall. I should have swallowed my pride and accepted the ride, but that would require me outing myself and the secret I don't want him to know. Pride is an admirable trait, but it can also be a person's downfall, and I suspect it will one day cost me more than I can imagine.

As expected, when I arrive at the shelter, there is no room for me. Not knowing what to do, I wonder about a block from the shelter until I spot an alleyway between a dry cleaner and a liquor store. About twenty feet into the alley is a dumpster, and beside the dumpster is a pile of old cardboard boxes. There is a small awning above where the cardboard lays that will do little to protect me from the snow when I sit on them. I need to find somewhere else to stay. There is a bridge on 42nd street, two blocks from here where the homeless gather. Perhaps I should make my way there for the night. The walk from work in the cold has taken its toll on me. I need to rest my feet a minute. They're throbbing and starting to go numb since I am not wearing socks or stockings.

After awhile, my body becomes tired and sluggish, so I decide to rest here a little longer. Huddled beside the dumpster, I prop myself against the brick wall behind me. With shaky hands, I dig through my bag, finding my wallet, then sift through what money I have, only producing fifty-seven dollars and some change, not enough for a hotel room. Stuffing my money back into the bag, I hug it against my chest as my sobs wrack my body. I have never felt so hopeless or as close to giving up in my life as I do at this moment. I should have taken the ride from Callan. I should have reached out for help instead of letting my pride get in the way. When you spend your entire life depending on nobody but yourself, asking for help becomes difficult. And with asking for help comes embarrassment and judgment that sometimes comes with the stigma surrounding homelessness.

Drawing my legs up to my chest, I lay on my side and tuck into myself as best I can. I'm going to rest for a moment longer. Then I'm going to get moving. The numbing cold is starting to become unbearable, so I do the only thing I know to do...count. Using my coping mechanism, I start at three thousand and count backward, my teeth chattering. "Two thousand nine hundred ninety-nine. Two thousand nine hundred ninety-eight." I lose count several times, and start over. My counting does little to help keep my mind off of the fact that the temperature is beginning to drop even more. Eventually, my words slur, my mind becomes a haze and my eyes grow heavy.

Time around me seems to stop as I start to doze off to sleep. Faintly hearing the voices of two men, I try with all the strength I can muster to open my eyes but fail. Then the voices become closer.

"Hey, Ricky. Look what we got over here."

"What is it, Henry?"

"Hey. Hey, there." Someone nudges me.

"What you got there, girl." I feel a tug on the bag clutched to my chest, and let out a groan as I try to keep hold of it, only my attempt is fruitless, and my backpack is ripped from my hands.

"She sure is a pretty little thing, isn't she Ricky?" I feel cold fingertips brush the side of my cheek.

"Come on, Henry. Let's take her bag and go before someone sees us."

I faintly hear a sigh, before the detached voice replies, "You're right. Let's go." The sound of shuffling feet and shoes crunching on freshly fallen snow echo as the two voices retreat. My eyes open to slits to see two men walking out of the alley. "Stop," I croak, but the men keep moving, their silhouettes disappearing amongst the foggy haze forming around me. I go to get up, but my body fails to budge. I'm briefly aware of the thin layer of snow that is now covering my body and my cold, damp hair sticking to the side of my face.

9

CALLAN

Grinding my teeth, I watch as Denver walks away, and an uneasy feeling settles in my gut. Her sudden change in attitude and lashing out was not like her. Granted, she was right. I didn't need her to stay. The fact is, I have this insane need to keep Denver close. That woman has gotten under my skin, and I am powerless to stop the overwhelming urge to want her and have her within arm's reach at all times. It's taken all my strength not to touch her, kiss her and fuck her against the wall of my office anytime she is in my presence. There is no logic to my choices. I'm selfish. I know Lucas has his sights set on Denver, which is why I stepped in and squashed his plans of asking her out. It's also the sole reason I turned into a bigger asshole this afternoon, making her stay. The moment Denver insisted she couldn't work late and had plans, I saw red. I became green with jealousy. But something about the way she handed me my ass and took off in tears doesn't sit right with me. I never meant to upset her. Something else must be going on. And I'm going to find out what the hell that is.

Still standing in the cold, snow accumulating on the shoulders of my coat, I eye Mitch. For the past few moments, he has patiently stood by the car with a worried look on his face, his eyes trained on the now-empty street. "Find her." I climb into the back seat, slamming the door.

"Yes, Sir." Mitch hurries around the front of the car and climbs into the driver's seat. Checking for traffic, he does a U-turn and drives us in the direction Denver disappeared.

"Fuck, she's gone. Do you see any sign of her, Mitch?" Mitch brings the car to crawl as I roll down the window.

"No. Sir. I don't see her."

Taking my phone from my pocket, I pull up Denver's contact and address information. I emailed her file to myself the day she started working. "Take me to 8279 West Chapel Rd," I tell Mitch.

Twenty minutes later, we pull up in front of a shitty apartment building in a shady rundown neighborhood. Anger bubbles inside at the thought of Denver living in a place like this.

Flinging the car door open, I take off in a jog up the steps of the apartment building with Mitch directly behind me. Mitch is a good man and has my back in case we run into any trouble. Ignoring the drunken men loitering in the hall, I make my way up to the third floor. As I reach apartment 59, I stop, lift my fist and pound on the door. Feeling impatient, I bang a little harder. This time a gruff male voice calls out from behind the door, and my already sour mood turns murderous. "Hold on a damn minute. I'm comin'." The door bursts open. A plump man with greasy hair and a cigarette hanging from his mouth stands before us. "What the hell do you want?"

"I'm looking for Denver."

"Who the hell is Denver?" the guy mumbles, and I watch cigarette ashes fall down the front of his shirt.

"The young woman who lives here, " I growl, taking a step forward, ready to beat the stranger's face in.

"Look, asshole. There ain't no Denver living here."

I take a step further into the man's face. "You sure?"

The man cranes his head to look at me. "I'd know if I had some bitch named Denver living here." The second the word 'bitch' leaves the guy's mouth, I lunge. Mitch stops me.

"He's not worth it, boss."

"You'd better listen to your buddy, pretty boy. Ain't no piece of ass worth you getting your ass handed to you," the fucker says, smirking. My fist makes direct contact with his nose, crunching against my knuckles. His sorry ass teeters on his heels, the smug smile wiped from his face, as I watch his body slump to the floor.

"Let's get out of here, boss before someone calls the cops." I let Mitch pull me away. As soon as we're inside the car, he peers in the rearview mirror. "We'll find her."

We drive around for hours, searching for any signs of Denver. The weather has taken a turn for the worse, and snow is falling heavily. Where the hell did she go? Furthermore, I don't understand why she would falsify her contact information. I start to worry she's in some kind of trouble. An ex maybe? Would she be hiding from a man? Perhaps she's been in trouble with the law? I know every scenario running through my head aren't good ones, but they are the only thoughts that come to mind. Keeping my eyes trained out the window, I keep searching, hoping we will find a clue to her whereabouts.

Two men exiting an alleyway up ahead catch my attention, and I follow them for a moment. Something reflective catches the streetlight on the object one of the men is carrying in his hand. It causes me to look closer. Wait a minute. I recognize the heart-shaped keychain attached to the bag. "Stop the fucking car!" I shout, throwing the door open. "Hey!" I yell at the men ahead of me as I barrel through the slush and snow toward them. "Hey, you!" The man with the bag in his hand takes off running, and I give chase. I tackle the other guy to the ground, as the one I was after disappears around the corner.

"What the fuck, man. Get the hell off of me."

"Where the fuck did your buddy get that backpack?" Gripping his jacket, I give him a shake.

"Screw you," he spews. I hear Mitch roll the car up beside me, and the door opens.

"Need me to call the police?" Mitch asks.

"No, no, no." The man in my grasp squirms. "No cops."

I look down at him. "Where did your friend get the bag?" I ask him one final time.

"We took it off some redheaded homeless bitch in the alley over there," he points, and I follow where he directs us. *Denver?* Letting him go, I get to my feet. Wasting no more of my time on the piece of shit, I sprint down the sidewalk, cutting into the alley. Straining my eyes to see in the dark, I finally spot an outline of what looks like a person, huddled between a dumpster and the building wall. As I approach, I make out her long red hair. "Shit." My heart sinks.

10

DENVER

Suddenly, I hear tires screeching and the thud, thud, thud of shoes hitting pavement until the sound of heavy breathing hovers directly above my cold body, followed by a string of curse words.

"Fucking motherfucker." I know that voice.

Next, a pair of strong hands reach beneath me, and lift my body from the ground. I find warmth as my cheek rests against something soft yet hard. I recognize that smell too. And when my cold nose nuzzles against a warm neck, I inhale. I get lost in the familiar scent and my nerves instantly calm, feeling safe.

"Is she alright, Mr. Hawk? You want to take her to the hospital?"

"No. Take us home, Mitch. Call Dr. Morgan. Tell him to meet us at my Penthouse."

At the slam of a car door, I tip my head back and open my eyes to see an intense pair of green eyes staring back at me. "Callan." His name manages to slip past my lips as I fight to stay awake.

"I've got you, baby."

Those are the last words I hear spoken before I'm thrusted into a dreaded pool darkness.

I WAKE FEELING WARM. Warm and nuzzled in the softest blanket known to mankind. I moan as I bury my face deeper into the pillow, taking in its fresh, clean scent. It takes a few seconds for my senses to come rushing back. This blanket is too soft. The ones at the shelter have never felt this good. Awareness dawns on me, my body stiffens, and I bolt upright, causing the blanket to pool around my waist. I gasp when I realize my bare breasts are exposed, and quickly yank the blanket up, covering myself. My eyes take in my unfamiliar surroundings. The bedroom I am currently in is enormous. To my right are floor to ceiling windows. The only thing visible through it is the moon as it shines through the room, illuminating the grey walls in a soft glow.

Scanning the rest of the bedroom, movement out of the corner of my eye has my head turning in that direction. A scream escapes my mouth at the shadowy figure sitting in a chair in the far corner of the room. I clutch my chest, drawing in a deep breath, but soon realize it's Mr. Hawk.

That's when my memories come flooding back. The alley. The freezing cold. The two men stealing my bookbag, the very bag carrying my only possessions: my ID, clothes and what little money I had. And finally, the memory of being scooped up into Mr. Hawk's arms. "What's going on? What am I doing here, and whose bed am I in?"

"I brought you here, and you are in my home and that is my bed." Mr. Hawk's voice is eerily calm as he takes a sip of the dark liquid from the tumbler in his hand.

I take a shuttered breath, asking my next question. "Why am I naked?"

"I undressed you," he answers.

"Mr. Hawk..."

"Callan," he cuts me off. "I want you to call me by my name." I pull the blanket tighter around my body and swallow.

"Where are my clothes, Callan?"

"I threw them in the trash."

"Why would you do that!" I cry. "And, why would you find the need to strip me of my clothing in the first place?"

"I undressed you because you were on the brink of hypothermia. I threw them in the trash because that's where they belong. I'll buy you new clothes." his voice raises with irritation. As if I shouldn't be asking all these questions.

"Those are the only clothes I own, Callan. You had no right to throw them away!"

Callan rises from his chair, turns as he throws his glass across the room, and it shatters against the wall, landing in tiny shards on the wood floor of his bedroom. "I had every right!" he booms, his chest heaving. "Tell me," he demands, taking a step in my direction.

"Tell you what?" I try not to shrink away from his looming presence as he approaches.

"Tell me why I found you nearly frozen to death on the city street."

"I...I think you have figured that out by now."

"I want to hear you say it, Denver. No more hiding."

Tears start to stream down my face, and I begin to shake.

"Why, Denver?"

"Because I didn't have anywhere to go!" I sob. "Because I'm homeless and the shelter was full. That's why I was sleeping in the alley. That's why I put up a fight when you wanted me to stay late at work. I knew if I stayed, I'd have zero chance at getting a bed for the night. If you had just let me leave when I was supposed to, none of this would have happened. I don't need your charity. I don't belong here."

"You are exactly where you should be." Callan takes another

step. "Where you don't belong is in a shelter. And you sure as hell don't belong sleeping in a fucking alley beside a dumpster and a pile of garbage, Denver."

"Why are you doing all of this, Callan? You're my boss and most of the time, I don't think you even like me. Now, suddenly, you care? Then, you follow me, bring me to your home, and take my clothes off." I pull at my hair in frustration. "Jesus! There aren't enough words to describe how messed up this situation is. I mean, I woke up naked. In my boss's bed."

"As I said before, you are right where you belong." Callan closes the distance between us, leans down to where his face is inches away from mine. "And I like you just fine, Denver."

Callan's whiskey scented breath washes over my face with his declaration, and I lick my lips. My anger seems to diminish the longer he holds my stare. His nose flares, and for a moment I think he's going to kiss me. I want him to. I want his lips pressed against mine so badly I hold my breath waiting for it to happen, only he doesn't.

Disappointment settles in my stomach as he backs away, putting space between us. I instantly miss his warmth when he does so. There is something about this man that makes me feel safe and at home. He infuriates me, yet at the same time, I find myself wanting him more and more each day that passes. Which is something I can't explain since we hardly know each other. The only Callan I know is the gruff asshole I work for. This Callan, well, he's still an asshole but is also strangely possessive of me, and my wellbeing. This side of him has my head spinning and my stomach doing somersaults all at the same time. I'd be lying if I said I didn't like it.

"Why don't you take a hot bath? There's shampoo, conditioner and lotion I had picked up for you on the bathroom counter," Callan nods toward the door behind him. "I also had some clothes brought over. They're in the closet."

How long was I asleep?

"Dinner should be here by the time you finish."

With that, Callan turns and walks out of the bedroom, shutting the door behind him, leaving me more confused than I was moments ago.

Tossing the sheet and blanket aside, I climb out of the most comfortable bed I have ever slept in. As I do, a sickening thought comes to mind, and my lip curls in disgust. How many times has he had sex with Joslyn in this very bed? Just thinking about that woman sets me off, and I fist the bedsheets in anger. Pushing those thoughts away, I pad across the room to the en-suite bathroom. My eyes widen when I flick the light on and take in how massive it is. It's almost as big as the bedroom itself. The bathtub is what dreams are made of. Sitting on the counter is an array of lotions, soaps, bubble bath, shampoo, and hair conditioner. There are also some razor blades and an unopened pack of toothbrushes.

Feeling overwhelmed, I choose the honey lavender bubble bath, twist the cap off and lift the bottle to my nose. *We have a winner.*

As I stride across the bathroom toward the tub, I catch a glimpse of my naked reflection in the large mirror on the wall beside the shower. Turning, I take a long look at myself. My hair is a knotted mess, still somewhat tied back in its braid. Removing the tie, my long red hair falls in loose curls around my waist. Deciding I need to wash it, I opt to take a quick shower before relaxing in the tub. But first, I pour some bubble bath in the tub and let it fill while I wash the grime and six months of stress from my body. After I finish, I step out of the shower and into the tub, moaning at how wonderful the hot water feels soaking into my skin. It's been so long since I enjoyed the luxury of a bath.

I don't know how long I stay immersed beneath the scented bubbles, but I don't get out until the water turns cold.

Wrapping a towel around my body, I make my way back over

to the counter, taking advantage of the hairdryer I spotted earlier. By the time I'm finished drying my long hair, it appears shiny and full of volume for the first time in ages. Next, I apply a generous amount of lotion, covering my entire body from head to toe.

Moving out of the bathroom and to Callan's walk-in closet where he said he had some clothes for me, I open the double doors. The moment I step in, a motion sensor is tripped, lighting up the shelves lining the walls. "Holy crap," I gasp. On one side, there is a row of neatly pressed suits. On the back wall is a very well organized shoe rack, and directly in the middle of the closet are many sets of cufflinks and watches laid out on a center table. To my left are several articles of women's clothing, the tags still attached. Spying a red sweater hanging from the rack, I flip the card over, revealing the price. My eyes nearly pop out of my head. "Three hundred dollars! For a sweater?" That man is out of his mind. Shaking my head, I look through the neatly folded pile of clothes on the shelf below the sweater, coming across a pair of white satin pajama pants and matching spaghetti strap top with a white satin robe. Looking around, I don't notice any undergarments. No way am I going commando. I open the drawer attached to the shelf in front of me, finally finding what I am looking for. There must be at least a dozen bras and panties here, and all in my size.

How did he know my size?

At that thought, I blush. Callan admitted to taking my clothes off. Not only did he see my pathetic excuse for a bra and my threadbare underwear, but he was also the first man ever to see me naked. For a moment, I wonder what his thoughts were when he was stripping me, and my most private parts were exposed to him.

Snapping myself out of my musings, I go about getting dressed, slipping the satin top over my head. The material is cold on my flushed body and feels like butter on my skin. Next, I step into a pair of white lace panties, followed by the pajama bottoms.

With my nipples on full display, I make use of the robe, doing my best to hide them.

By the time I finish, my stomach lets out a loud rumble. Callan did say he was getting dinner. Only my nerves kick in and I become reluctant to leave the room. I'm not sure what faces me beyond the bedroom door. I've been out of my element the moment I woke up in his bed. I'm confused as to what Callan's end game is. He said this is where I belong, but what did he mean by that? Is it his intention to help me out for the night then send me on my way tomorrow?

I sigh. "Go out there and confront him, Denver. Quit being a chicken."

The smell of Chinese food permeates through the apartment, making my stomach growl again and I step out of the bedroom into a hallway. There is a faint light at the end of the hall, and I pad in that direction, coming to a stop when I see Callan shuffling around the kitchen. He's changed out of his suit and is now wearing a pair of well-worn jeans and a black shirt. Sensing my presence, he calls me. "Come here, Denver." The smooth timbre of his voice makes me shiver. "Sit." Callan nods to the stool at the kitchen island. Not once does he take his eyes off me as I make my way to him. Those green orbs run the length of my body. The intensity in which he stares has me thinking back to my earlier thoughts—thoughts of how the man in front of me has seen all my lady bits, and the look on his face tells me he's thinking the same.

I take a seat on the stool, remaining silent as Callan starts scooping rice and chicken onto two plates. My leg bounces, and I wring my hands in my lap as I try to calm my nerves.

"Relax, baby," Callan says, his tone gentle.

"I...I can't."

"Why?" he asks while continuing his task, and I blurt out the only thing currently on my brain.

"You saw me naked!" I clasp my hand over my mouth and my cheeks heat.

"It was either Dr. Morgan or me," he growls, "and no fucking way was I allowing another man to see you." Callan shrugs, his admission further confusing me. Setting a plate of food in front of me, he points, "Eat."

I think about defying him merely because his bossiness is getting on my nerves; my growling stomach chooses otherwise.

The two of us eat together in silence, and when I'm halfway through my meal, I ask, "Callan, since you threw my clothes in the garbage, will it be okay if I take a few of the things hanging in the closet when I leave? I can pay you back when I get my next check."

Callan grits his teeth. "You can have everything in there. I bought them for you, but you won't be leaving, Denver. You're going to stay here."

I choke on the rice I've just shoved in my mouth. "What? Me... live here?"

"Was I not clear before when I said you are where you belong?"

"Uh...Not really, Callan. You're not very good at explaining details. Listen, I can't live here with you. I don't need your charity. Besides, what would Joslyn say about me staying here?"

"Joslyn has no say in what I do."

Callan's dismissal of the facts makes me angry. "So, what? You won't tell your girlfriend you moved another woman in with you? Am I some dirty secret or something? The poor pathetic homeless woman who works for you; who needs your help? Well, let me tell you something, Callan Hawk, I don't need your help and I damn sure won't be some secret you keep from your girlfriend. I may not like the woman, but I'm no homewrecker," I fume.

"First off." Callan moves around the kitchen island and twists the stool I am currently perched on until we are face to face. "If I ever hear you talk shit like that about yourself again, I'm going to put you over my knee. You are not pathetic, and you sure as fuck are not a dirty secret. Second, Joslyn is not and never was my girl-friend. Joslyn was nothing more than someone I used to pass the time with. All that stopped the day you walked into my office."

I flinch at his admission. "What do you mean? As I recall, she made several appearances since I started working for you. She also took pleasure in making snarky jabs toward me. All while you sat there and did nothing." I don't bother hiding the hurt in my voice.

"I ended things with Joslyn right after she made those comments too. I told her I didn't want to see her again. Her showing up at my office after that day was not me wanting her there, it was her not wanting to give up the fact she had been sent packing. Joslyn is an opportunist. She thinks I don't know why she was with me. I'm no fool. Joslyn has been a part of my life off and on for four years and is mad because I refused to define our rela-tionship and give her the status she desperately wanted."

At a loss for words, I stay silent as I try to absorb what Callan is saying.

"I don't do girlfriends, Denver. Or at least I didn't before. That's about to change." Callan pauses, puts his finger beneath my chin, and brings my eyes to his. "Do you get what I'm saying, baby?"

I shake my head. My heart rate picks up and my breath gets caught in my throat.

"You can't deny the pull between us, Denver. It's been there since the first day. I can feel it, and I know you can feel it. I'm telling you now, there will be no more fighting what's between us," Callan vows just before his mouth covers mine.

Callan's kiss starts soft and sweet. When his tongue licks the seam of my lips, I open, granting him access. The moment his tongue tangles with mine, I moan and my body melts into his. Wrapping his arms around my waist, he reaches behind my back, grabs hold of my long hair, tilts my head back and dominates my mouth. The kiss quickly turns to something more powerful. Fisting my hands in Callan's shirt, I pull him closer, desperate to feel his body heat. With our bodies flush against one another, there is no mistaking the rigid length currently pressed against my belly and how much our kiss is affecting him as well.

Releasing his hold on my hair, Callan brings his hands up and cups my face in his palms. When I open my eyes, I'm met by his mossy green stare. "Does that clear a few things up for you?"

"I think so."

11

DENVER

I wake the next morning feeling warm, and the sun's light shining on my face. My cheek is currently pressed against a hard chest, and one of my legs is draped over one of Callan's thighs. The moment I attempt to move, a strong arm wraps around my middle, keeping me in place. Feeling totally out of my element, I try pulling away once more, and his arm tightens. Callan's warm breath skirts across the side of my face. "Relax, baby."

Relax? How am I supposed to relax when I've never slept next to a man before? I was alone going to bed last night. Callan said he would crash on the couch. "Uh...Callan?"

"Hmm?"

"Why are you in bed with me? You were supposed to sleep on the couch. If that was a problem, you could have said something, and I would have traded places with you."

"I won't have you sleeping on the damn couch. I checked on you a few times, finding you restless, so I waited until you finally fell asleep before climbing into bed."

"Why?"

Callan nuzzles his nose in the crook of my neck. "Because of how you're acting now. I knew you'd freak out when I only wanted to comfort you. I had no other intentions than wanting to make you feel safe and not alone."

"I'm not freaking out," I lie. I'm totally freaking out. Callan's chuckle tells me he knows I'm full of crap.

"Baby," his voice vibrates in his chest.

Oh god. There's that word again.

"Even in sleep, your body knows what it wants. That's why as soon as I laid down in the bed, you tucked your body close to mine. Right where it belongs."

"I did not!"

Callan chuckles again. "Baby. You slept on me all night and didn't move an inch."

I open and close my mouth, looking for a reason to protest. "I'm so embarrassed."

"Nothing to be embarrassed about." Callan starts stroking my hair.

"I think things are moving a little too fast."

"I don't think so."

"Callan." I breathe a sigh of frustration as I move away from him. This time he doesn't stop me.

Callan climbs out of bed, revealing he's wearing nothing but a pair of white boxer briefs, fitting him so well, they leave nothing to the imagination. I don't know how long I've been staring at Callan's impressive package, but it was long enough for me to miss whatever he just said.

"My eyes are up here, Denver." Callan's amusement is evident.

I snap my head up, feeling my cheeks heat. "What?"

"I said I'm going to make some breakfast. Would you like coffee?"

"Oh. Yeah," I stumble over my words. "Coffee and food." Callan tries suppressing a smile, clearly amused.

Suddenly, I remember what day it is. "We're going to be late for work!" I leap from the bed, and rush toward the bathroom.

"Denver, relax. We're working from home today."

I stop in my tracks. "Can we do that?"

"I'm the boss, remember. I can do whatever the hell I want."

"Why are we staying ho...I mean here?" I still can't let myself wholeheartedly believe what Callan said last night, about being where I belong.

Callan finishes pulling on his sweatpants and strides up to me, cupping my face. "I want you to say it, Denver."

"Say what?"

"Home." His eyes search mine. "This is home, baby."

I bite my bottom lip, not sure about this entire situation. Can I trust Callan? Does he mean all the words he has spoken? I search his eyes, looking for deception. Trying to find a single reason, or feeling why I shouldn't trust him. This whole thing is insane, but I find the word leaving my lips on a whisper. "Home."

Fifteen minutes later, after taking care of business in the bathroom, I dress in a pair of jeans, which fit me perfectly and the red sweater I spotted the night before. Then, follow my nose to the kitchen, where I find a shirtless Callan standing over the stove.

"Something smells good."

"You like eggs?" he asks over his shoulder, where he pauses to drink in the sight of me. "You look amazing, as always."

As always? I find it hard to believe Callan Hawk thinks I look amazing. Nevertheless, his compliment has an effect on me. Ducking my head, I tuck a lock of hair behind my ear. "Thanks. You'll have to tell whoever picked the stuff out I said thank you," I say tugging on the hem of the sweater.

"That would be Maggie, my stylist. I'll tell her you said thank you. She'll be stopping by tomorrow with some more stuff."

"Callan, no. You've already done too much. Please. I don't need anything else."

"I want to do this for you, Denver. It's not enough. You deserve more." The grip on the spatula in his hand tightens and the set line of Callan's jaw tells me this is not an argument I'm going to win.

"So, who taught you how to cook?" I say, sitting in one of the stools at the kitchen island.

Callan's body relaxes, and he smiles. "My mom."

"Where does she live? Here in the city?"

"No. She passed away."

"Oh. Callan, I'm so sorry."

He shrugs. "It was a long time ago. Anyway, she was a single mom who worked two jobs to make ends meet. I had to learn to cook. Mom wasn't always home in time to make a hot meal. When I was old enough, she taught me how to make a few dishes."

"Well, I think that's pretty special. Now every time you make those things, it's like having a piece of your mom with you."

Turning the fire beneath the skillet off, Callan transfers the eggs to the plates next to him on the countertop. After buttering some toast, he turns, then sets my meal in front of me.

A few minutes later, Callan and I are in the middle of eating breakfast, when we are interrupted by a knock on the door. Callan stands. "That's probably Lucas. I asked him to bring some files from the office." Not wanting anyone at work to know what's going on with Callan and me, I make a move to get up.

Callan senses I'm about to flee to the other room and barks. "Stay."

"Callan," I hiss. "I don't want Lucas to know I'm here."

Callan grinds his teeth hisses. "Why is that?" If I didn't know any better, I would say Callan is jealous of Lucas. Looking back, that would explain his behavior toward Lucas anytime he and I were around each other.

"The last thing I want is for people to gossip about us; me

specifically. I don't want to become a cliché. You know, the whole secretary sleeping with the boss."

"I don't give a fuck who knows about us. Least of all, Lucas."

I take a second to ponder Callan's response. Something about it causes a warning light to go off in my brain. "Wait a minute. Why did you want Lucas to bring you what you needed? Why not Frances or anybody else?"

When Callan doesn't answer, I narrow my eyes at him. "You did this on purpose. You wanted him to see me here with you. Is this your way of pissing on me or something?"

"If that's what you want to call it, baby." Callan shrugs. "I call it a man making it known to another man, what belongs to him." Callan's caveman rant spews from his mouth just as there is another knock at the door. Without another word, he turns and answers. Only it's not Lucas standing there; it's Kelly. Great. Kelly showing up is worse. There is no telling what kind of crap she's going to spread around the office. Especially since she's had it out for me since the moment I started working there.

Kelly's annoying voice rings out. "Hello, Mr. Hawk. I have those files you asked for." So far, Callan's large frame blocks Kelly's view of me.

"Why are you bringing them and not Lucas as I asked?" Callan's voice carries a hint of irritation. Folding my arms across my chest, I smirk. Serves him right for trying to be a jerk.

"Lucas got tied up down at the courthouse, so I volunteered to bring you what you needed." The flirtation of Kelly's voice has me rolling my eyes.

"I bet you did," I mumble under my breath. Just then, Callan shuffles to the left, placing the documents on the table beside the door.

"What the hell is Denver doing here?" she screeches while pointing an accusing finger in my direction. Kelly makes eye contact with me, her face red, and her eyes like daggers.

"Denver is none of your concern. If I were you, Kelly, I'd tread lightly. You are my employee, not someone who shows up on my doorstep asking personal questions. Now, if you'll excuse us, we have breakfast to finish and you have a job to get back to." Callan shuts the door in Kelly's angry, shocked face. Not giving a damn, I do nothing to hide the smile that takes over mine.

"I changed my mind. I don't care who knows I'm here. Any rumors that go around the office will be worth it because of what you just did."

Callan strolls back into the kitchen, and sits down. "Kelly needed to learn her place."

"Kelly just wants in your pants." My thoughts spill from my mouth.

"You jealous, baby?" Callan smirks and I roll my eyes.

"No!"

"Liar." He has no problem calling me out.

"Whatever. You know I'm right."

"Just like Lucas wants to fuck you. Which, by the way, will never fucking happen."

"Callan," I sigh. "Lucas and I are only friends. I don't want to sleep with him." I level him with a look.

"That doesn't mean he's not going to try. The only man getting a taste of your pussy will be me."

Callan says his last statement the same moment I take a swallow of coffee, causing the warm liquid to spew from my mouth all over him and the kitchen island between us. "You can't say things like that!" My face heats.

"Facts, baby. Only speaking facts." Callan retrieves a dish towel from a drawer near the stove, and begins drying himself.

Feeling a bit awkward, and not sure what to say, I remain seated, collecting my thoughts for a moment. I'm staring at my plate, pushing what's left of my eggs around with my fork. Placing a fresh mug of coffee in front of me, Callan sits, and resumes eating his meal. "Callan," I decide to speak what is currently on my mind. "You don't know me. Not well enough to say such personal things."

"I know enough to realize what I want." He places his fork on his almost empty plate, and focuses solely on me. " And I want you."

I lean back in my chair. "Other than bringing you coffee, taking notes, and scheduling your dry cleaning, you and I know nothing about one another." Needing space, I stand. "You're moving way too fast for me, Callan."

Pushing himself from the counter, Callan makes his way toward me. Drawn to him, I take a step forward. He brushes my hair from my shoulder, and his fingertips graze the side of my neck just below my ear, causing my skin to prickle. "You telling me you want to ignore this pull between us, and the way your body reacts to my touch?" His hand falls as he runs his palm down my arm, before settling his hands on my waist

"I'm not denying anything." I swallow hard, trying to ignore the pounding of my heart. Before I have a chance to say more, Callan leans down, and kisses my forehead. I close my eyes as his lips linger for a moment, and completely forget what I was about to say.

"Good. Glad we're on the same page." Stepping back, taking his warmth and touch with him, Callan places our dishes in the sink.

I finally blink. Forehead kisses must be this man's superpower. How can one simple action have left me mute?

Later that evening, I'm lying on the couch with my head resting on a pillow after spending most of the day lazing around watching Callan work on his laptop and make phone calls. "How did you know where to find me last night?" I don't know why I haven't asked this question already.

Closing his laptop, Callan sets it on the table in front of him. "I had my driver turn around and attempt to follow you. You were so angry about having to stay late after work, and it continued to nag at me. At first, I thought you were acting irrationally, but quickly realized that's not you. In the weeks you have worked for me, not once have you complained." Callan shakes his head. "My gut was telling me something was off. I told myself to at least see you got home okay. By the time I had the driver turn around to find you, you were gone. We drove around for a bit, until I caught sight of two men walking from between the two buildings where we found you. I wouldn't have given them a second thought until I recognized the bag in one man's hand to be yours."

MY MIND DRIFTS back to the vague awareness of the men Callan may be referencing. "I remember hearing voices." I drop my eyes to my lap, "Whoever they were, they had stolen the only possessions I owned."

Callan clears his throat, and scoots to the edge of the sofa, leaning his elbows on his knees. "I don't want to be presumptuous, but why not get a hotel when you found you couldn't stay at the shelter?"

I hang my head. "I had found an apartment. It wasn't in a good neighborhood, but I liked it well enough. The guy who claimed to be the apartment manager seemed nice enough too." I wring my hands together, and sigh. "Anyway, I went back the next day with the key, ready to move in, only to find he wasn't the manager. He had taken my money and skipped town. I left with no money and no apartment. It's my fault really for being so stupid."

"It is not your fault you were taken advantage of, Denver. You're far from stupid," Callan growls, his anger over my admission apparent. Standing, Callan makes his way to the bar at the corner of the living room and fixes a tumbler of whiskey. "Tell me your story, Denver. I want to know everything there is to know about you. The real you." I watch him pour a small amount of white wine into a glass, before walking back to the sofa and handing it to me. Callan sits beside me, relaxing into the back cushion, and takes a sip of his drink.

Sitting up on the couch, I run my sweaty palm up and down my thighs. I don't trust easily, but with Callan, I feel I can trust him with all the ugly parts of me.

"Tell me about your family. How did you end up homeless?" Several questions slip from Callan's lips.

I take a sip of the wine he handed me and think back to the last memory, one of the only memories I have of my mother. "My mother was beautiful. One of the few memories I have seems more like a polaroid picture that I keep filed away for safekeeping." Closing my eyes, I see her standing out in the rain on a sunny day, with her face lifted to the sky. "From what I can remember, I look a lot like her; long red hair, fair skin, the same blue eyes." Sadness washes over me. "She seemed to be sad all the time."

"What about your father? Remember anything about him?"

I shake my head. "Nothing. I have no recollection of him." My mind drifts back to the final moment I shared with my mother, and the last memory she left me with. Dropping my head, I stare at the wine glass in my hand and run my fingertip around the thin rim. That day plays like snippets of a pieced together home movie as I try to explain. "I was almost five years old, or at least that's what I was told. I remember sitting on a wooden bench in a hall-way, and my mother kneeled in front of me." I feel tears stream down my face. "Be a good girl for mommy and stay right here. Can you do that for me?" I repeat the final words my mother spoke to me. I continue, "I nodded, smiling at her. Then remember reaching out, brushing my tiny fingertips over the freckles on her face. My mom smiled back at me, but her eyes held the same sadness they always did as she told me she loved me."

"Baby," Callan says sympathetically, and I give him a brief smile and a shrug.

"I watched her walk down that long hallway as I played with the tattered dolly in my lap. She turned one final time, smiling at me before she disappeared around the corner." I pull in a shuddered breath. "That was the last time I saw her. She left me there and never came back. Turns out, the Children's Home she left me at that day, would become my home for a while until I started getting shuffled from one foster home to another." I take another sip of wine and pull in a deep breath to collect myself.

"Did you ever learn why your mother left you there that day?" Callan questions, and I wish I had the answer to give him.

"No. And I've never had the means or resources to find out on my own."

"And there's nothing more you can remember?" The genuine concern in his voice warms my heart.

"Nothing." I pause. "Maybe it's just my mind's way of protecting myself." I lift my eyes to Callan's. "I never had time to feel sad for myself, and I won't start now. My memory of my mother may not be the best, but I do know I loved her, and she loved me. I felt it that day. My life has never been easy, but I've survived, Callan."

After a few moments of sitting in silence, I continue to tell him the rest of my story, telling him about all the foster homes I experienced throughout my childhood and teen years—how I became homeless. I dumped it all on him, sharing everything as he sat silently next to me, listening to every word. Turns out, purging my thoughts and life story proved to be therapeutic. "It was Lucas's grandfather who helped me get the job as your assistant. He helped me fill out applications and everything. It was the first time in a long time someone had been so nice to me." I feel my eyes water, but hold back my emotions and continue. "At first, I said no. I never thought I'd get the job in the first place. Then I came in for my interview and met Frances." I smile. "I was sitting in a chair right outside your office. You came out and didn't even see me sitting there. You walked past me as if I were invisible, and kept right on going."

"Baby," Callan sits his glass of whiskey on the coffee table, then drops to his knees in front of me. "I'm so fucking sorry I did that."

"Oh, Callan. I'm not saying this to make you feel guilty. I'm telling you this, so you understand where I'm coming from. I want you to understand my perspective of things. I've been overlooked my whole life. Growing up in the system has made it clear that it's easier for people to pretend people like me don't exist rather than fix the problems and how the system fails many of us every day. Roland was the first person in a very long time to look at me and treat me like I was human, just like him. Then, there is you. The way you look at me. You don't see through me anymore like you did that first day. It feels like you see inside me, and it scares the crap out of me, Callan. I'm afraid to trust it—in you." Those last two words cause Callan to flinch a little. "I'm afraid that we are rushing into things. That you will wake up tomorrow and realize I am not what you want; that I am not good enough."

Callan cups my face and wipes the tears flowing down my cheeks. "I see you." He gently kisses me before he takes my bottom lip between his teeth. "You are so fucking beautiful. I see you, baby."

12

DENVER

The kiss progresses into more in a matter of seconds. Warm hands snake up the inside of my sweater and Callan's thumbs brush over my nipples, causing me to shiver. "Callan," I gasp.

Still seated on the couch with Callan kneeling on the floor in front of me, I wrap my legs around his waist, drawing his body closer to mine. Pushing forward, Callan's hard cock comes into contact with the space between my legs, causing me to moan. "Oh, God."

"It feels good, doesn't, baby?"

"Yes. So good," I shamelessly admit.

Gripping the bottom of my sweater, Callan pulls it up, past my ribs, and I raise my arms, allowing him to remove it from my body. He tosses it to the floor while drinking in the sight of me wearing a black lace bra.

Leaning forward, Callan doesn't waste any time cupping my right breast with one hand and latching his hot mouth onto my laced covered nipple, while his other hand works the strap of my bra on the other side. Gently, he slips it over my shoulder and down my arm. When his mouth releases my nipple, he makes work of the other strap, sliding it down, exposing both breasts. My breathing picks up, and so do my nerves. This is happening. "Callan. I..."

"Do you want me to stop?"

I don't hesitate to tell him, "No."

"We're going to take this slow. We only go as far as you want it to go," he assures me.

My nerves settle, and my body relaxes. "I want this. I do. It's just, I've never done this and I'm not sure..."

"I'm sure enough for the both of us, baby. All you need to do is let me take care of you."

I nod. "Okay."

Callan cups both breasts in his large hands. "I've been dying to see these beautiful tits for weeks." His tongue darts out, flicking one of my taut nipples. Once he's done playing with one, he switches to the other, giving it equal attention. I arch my back and buck my hips when his teeth bite down on my sensitive flesh, causing my sex to clench and clit to throb.

"I'm going to take your pants off now, baby. You okay with that?"

I lick my lips. "Yes."

A predatory smile takes over Callan's face as he flicks the button on my jeans.

"Lay back, Denver." I do as I'm told and lay back against the couch. He then grips my jeans and tugs them over my hips and down my legs, leaving me in just my panties. His eyes darken when his gaze zeroes in on the space between my legs. "I can't wait to get my mouth on this pussy." Sliding his palms up my calves and in between my thighs, Callan spreads my legs wide. "Hold your legs open, Denver. Show me what's mine. Show me what no other man has had the pleasure of tasting or ever will." He inches his face a little closer, and I fight the urge to raise my hips. "Say it, baby. Say I'm the only man who will have this pussy," Callan demands, his nose flaring.

"Only you, Callan."

Hooking the scrap of material covering my pussy with his finger, he moves it aside, exposing me.

"Fucking perfect." The words barely leave his mouth before his tongue takes its first taste. Not expecting the pleasure to feel this exquisite, I scream out his name. "Callan!"

As if his name on my lips fuels his hunger for me, he lets out a primal growl, a rumbling from deep within his chest, as he rips the panties from my body. Clutching my ass in the palms of his hands, he brings my pussy to his mouth and feasts on me. Callan licks and nips at my center just before his tongue delves inside of me, taking all I have to give. That's it; that is all it takes for the pressure that has been building inside me to explode into his mouth. My orgasm rips through my soul as flashes of light dance behind my eyelids.

"Look at me, Denver. Open your eyes and watch." At his command, I open my eyes in time to watch as Callan reaches behind his neck, tugging his shirt off over his head, revealing the tattoo I've seen peeking through the collar of his dress shirts on several occasions. His tattoo is of two black and grey hawks. With them are the initials K.H. The design is intricate and spans his whole right shoulder and over his peck. If I had to guess, I'd say the tattoo is a representation of his last name. My eyes travel south to where he is lowering the zipper of his jeans and pulls them down just enough for his length to spring free. I look on, hypnotized at the way his hand works his cock.

Curious as to how it would feel in my hands, I ask, "Can I do it?"

"You never have to ask to touch me, baby."

Reaching between my spread legs, I wrap my hand around Callan's cock. It's hard, smooth, and just as big as I imagined. I watch as a pearl of pre-cum settles at the tip, and I swipe it with the pad of my thumb, my action causing him to hiss. "Squeeze it tight, baby. Just like that." I work his cock up and down, paying close attention to his reactions. "I'm about to come. Spread your legs wider and let me cum all over that pretty pussy."

Opening my legs wider, I continue stroking him, until the head of his cock swells. Callan lets out a throated growl as jets of cum spills, covering my sex. I swear I almost come again at the sight of his warm release coating my skin.

Not caring about the sticky mess between us, Callan pulls my body against his, and I wrap my legs around his hips once more. I glide my palms up and down his sweaty back and can't resist tilting my head back and kissing his neck. It doesn't take long before I feel his cock swell once again between us. And when Callan thrusts his hips forward, the tip brushes against my clit.

Needing more, I begin to grind myself against him, meeting him thrust for thrust, as his long thick cock continues to work my clit. "That's it. Come for me again. Come all over my cock." This time Callan doesn't allow my eyes to close when my orgasm hits for a second time. He grips my chin with one hand, while he holds my body flush against his with the other, forcing my eyes to stay on his as he too crashes over the edge.

THE NEXT MORNING, we are sitting in the back of his car on our way to the office, as I drown out Callan's voice while he barks orders over the phone. So much has happened and I feel like my brain has yet to catch up. First, there is Callan, who up until two days ago I thought didn't like me and merely tolerated my existence.

Now, he has declared me his, and has pretty much taken over my life. He's given me a place to live, and bought me clothes. My life has suddenly become a fairytale. There's a part of me that is still airing on the side of caution. Still leery to fully trust the whirlwind I'm caught up in. It feels as though this is all a dream and I'm going to wake up and be thrust back into the nightmare my life was before Callan plucked my weary body off the cold city street.

Before I know it, the car stops in front of Callan's building, and I find him looking at me expectantly while holding a large gift box with intricate lettering scrolled across the lid. "Callan..."

"I know what you're going to say, Denver, but I got it for you anyway. Please, baby. Take it." Callan places the box on my lap.

"This is too much, Callan. You've gotten me so much already. Much more than one person needs. To think how many people could be helped with the money you've spent on me in the past couple of days..."

"We can discuss those thoughts later. Please, open the box." Callan insists.

With shaky hands, I lift the lid to reveal a lavish handbag. My eyes widen in shock. "It's gorgeous Callan, but I can't accept this." I shake my head. "You don't have to buy me things like this. You know I would have been content with a twenty-dollar purse."

"I know you would. That's one of the reasons I got you this. Because you don't expect lavish gifts. The second reason is that you deserve the best. So, that is what you will get."

Turning back to the box on my lap, I pull the purse out and run my hands along the smooth feel of the leather. It is a beautiful bag. I've never held something so luxurious in my hands before. Then I feel guilty knowing the price he must have paid for it. His money would do better elsewhere, like helping out the people down at the shelter.

"I had Mitch pick you up a new ID," Callan nods toward his driver. "It's in the wallet."

Looking in the bag, I grab the wallet inside and open it. Sure enough, there is a new ID, along with a black credit card with the name Callan Hawk on it.

"What's this for?"

"It's yours to use however you want," Callan shrugs.

"I make my own money, Callan. I don't need it."

His face softens. "I know you do, baby. Keep it anyway, just in case."

"Fine," I huff.

Callan smiles, liking the fact he has won yet another battle, and I roll my eyes. "Come on, let's go." He grabs my hand as he goes to slide out of the car. I stop him.

"Why don't you go first. I'll wait a minute then come in behind you."

Callan's jaw ticks and he refuses to let go of my hand. "No. We will walk in together."

Not wanting to rehash the same discussion, I relent and allow Callan to help me from the car, leading me inside the building.

When we pass the security desk, the guard nods. "Mr. Hawk, Miss Hollis."

During the elevator ride up, I can't stop fidgeting. Callan squeezes my hand. "You're worried about nothing."

"Am I? The moment we step off the elevator, everyone will see us together. They will see the new clothes I'm wearing and the ten thousand-dollar handbag on my arm. I know what they will all think, Callan."

"I told you yesterday I don't give a fuck what people think. If any of them have the nerve to open their mouths, I'll fire their asses."

Callan turns to me and cups my face. "This thing between us is happening. I'm not hiding, and neither will you." He kisses my lips, and just like that, I melt against him.

Stepping off the elevator, the first person we run into is Kelly, who is already sitting at her desk. She looks at our joined hands then up at my face. She doesn't openly sneer at me because she wouldn't do such a thing in front of Callan. Especially since he handed her ass to her yesterday, I have no doubt she will give me hell the first chance Callan is out of earshot, but that doesn't stop me from giving her my best, 'he's mine' look while offering her a smug smile.

"I knew it!" Is France's response when Callan drops me off at my desk a few seconds later.

"Frances—" Callan tries to cut her off; only she doesn't listen.

"Although, I told Richard it would take you at least another two weeks before you broke." Frances beams and it's Callan's turn to roll his eyes.

"Who's Richard?" I ask.

"Richard is my husband," Frances supplies.

"He and I had a bet going on how long it would take Callan to accept he was smitten with you."

"I'll be in my office," Callan says, ignoring Frances, but doesn't hide his amusement.

"Coffee, Miss Hollis!" he calls out just before shutting his door.

At least some things haven't changed.

The morning passes without incident. It turns out I was worked up for nothing, and worried how people would treat me after word got around the office about the boss and me. Everyone I encountered acted as if it was just another day. All except Lucas, who gave me a knowing smirk when I ran into him while fixing Callan some coffee. As for Kelly, she has been surprisingly pleasant as well. She has even gone as far as to throw a couple smiles my way. I don't trust Kelly as far as I can throw her, and intend on growing a pair of eyes in the back of my head when it comes to her.

Callan and I missed our lunch together due to the fact he had court at 11:30. I accepted Frances's invitation to eat with her instead. "Are you going to spill and tell me what happened between you and Callan?" Frances grills the moment we sit down at the deli in the lobby. "Was it when he made you stay late the other night? I knew he was using it as a ruse to spend more time with you. He couldn't have been more obvious. Did he confess his feelings then?"

I swallow the bite of the turkey club I have in my mouth. "Not exactly." I wring my hands in my lap. "We fought when I declined his offer to give me a ride home." Frances looks at me with bewilderment. I continue, "I didn't want him to give me a ride because I didn't want him to know I was homeless and staying in a shelter."

"Oh, Denver. Why didn't you tell me? I could have helped."

"I know you would have helped, Frances. But I was too ashamed."

"Being homeless is nothing to be ashamed of, dear."

"It's not just that. I'm used to being on my own. Have been my whole life. I guess I've gotten used to not being able to depend on other people." I pause a moment thinking about Callan. "Callan is showing me I can trust people; I can let them help. He's been amazing to me."

"I'm happy he can be that person for you, Denver. Callan is one of the best men I know." I let her words settle with me as we finish our meal, and she doesn't pry into my personal business any further.

Arriving back at the office after lunch, I notice the door to Callan's office is closed. He must be back from court. Anxious to see how things went with Mrs. Dennis, I knock on the door twice before opening it. "Hey, Callan. I wanted to see..." I don't finish my sentence because what I see in front of me causes my words to catch in my throat. Joslyn currently has her arms wrapped around Callan's neck, their lips fused in a kiss. My heart feels like it has been ripped from my chest. All I can do is stand there, frozen in place. Callan makes eye contact with me just before I turn and run. I don't make it three feet past my desk before an arm snakes around my waist, and I'm pulled back against a hard chest. "Let me go," I croak, trying to push out of Callan's hold.

Callan pulls me closer, his mouth pressed against my ear. "Never."

Through my blurred vision, I catch sight of the security guard, making his way toward us. Callan barks, "Please escort Joslyn from the building and make sure she is not allowed back in. If she tries, have her arrested."

"Are you seriously having me kicked out, Callan?"

"Yes. I warned you the last time you were here not to come back."

"Why? Because of your little pet mouse?" Joslyn scoffs.

"No. Because you disrespected my woman and because you're an opportunistic bitch. Now get out." Keeping his hold on me, Callan doesn't spare Joslyn a second glance as he maneuvers me into his office. I wrap my arms around myself while refusing to meet his eyes. "Baby. What you saw was not what it looked like." I sniffle using the sleeve of my shirt to wipe my face. "I know." Callan puts his finger under my chin, tipping my head back.

"You believe me?" The look on his face is pure anguish.

"Yes. I didn't know at first. But the fact you had security escort her out tells me you didn't want her here. It doesn't make seeing her kiss you hurt any less, though."

"I'm sorry, Denver. She was here waiting in my office when I got back from court. I called security the second I saw her. I told her the last time she was here; she wasn't welcome back. Her pulling this stunt is the last straw. She had no reason to show up here today, considering I ended what we had weeks ago. I wasn't lying when I told you the other night Joslyn and I are done."

"I know. I believe you." My nerves start to calm.

"Good. I told you, Denver, I knew you were it for me your first day here."

"Oh. Well, you sure had a funny way of showing it sometimes," I grumble making light of the situation.

Callan kisses the pout right off my face. "What do you say we knock off early, pick up some takeout and go home?"

"I'd say that sounds like the perfect plan."

13

DENVER

Two weeks have passed, and the news of Callan and me has fizzled around the office. We have also picked up a routine. We ride into work together every morning, and aside from a stolen kiss here and there, we are focused on keeping a professional relationship at work, something I like. I've learned that Callan is passionate about his job and devoted to his clients. I've learned he is very much a homebody, preferring to stay home rather than go out to fancy restaurants and clubs.

It's Saturday morning, and the two of us are lounging in bed. Me with a book and Callan on his laptop. I have been working up the nerve the past couple of days to ask him about his family. Other than the brief conversation we had about his mom, he has yet to mention his father or whether or not he has any other relatives. I sense it's a touchy subject, but I find myself wanting to know all there is to know about the man I'm slowly starting to fall in love with.

Blowing out a breath, I close my book, sit up, and set it on the table beside the bed. Callan looks at me expectedly. "Something on your mind?"

"How come you don't talk about your dad? You've never mentioned brothers or sisters, so I am assuming you have none." Callan flexes his jaw, and for a second, I think I have crossed the line. "You don't have to tell me if you don't want to. I feel like I have given you all of me, yet I don't have all of you."

Callan's face softens at my admission. "You're right. My father is not a subject I like discussing." Callan sets his laptop to the side and scrubs his palm down his face. "My father left my mom and me when I was ten. And when he walked out the door, he left us with nothing."

"Oh, Callan. I'm so sorry."

"My father met my mom when he was on a business trip to Vegas. She was a waitress in the hotel restaurant he was staying in. According to her, their romance was a whirlwind. He swept her off her feet in one weekend. They were married three days after meeting, and I was born less than a year later. My mom quit her job, left her home, and moved to New York with my father. The thing I remember the most about him growing up is him hardly being home. I also remember how sad my mom was all the time when he was away, and how much they fought when he was home. Mom was good about keeping that part of their marriage hidden. When I was eight, I overheard one of their arguments. They were fighting because mom had accused my father of cheating. The fighting went on for another two years. Until one day, my father came home and announced right at the dinner table, he wanted a divorce and that he was giving my mom until the end of the month to find another place to live." Callan's features harden as he reflects on his past.

"Oh my god." I put my hand over my mouth. I imagine a ten year-old Callan sitting down for dinner with his family and his dad telling his mom they have to leave their home. "That's why you do what you do. Why you take on the cases you do?"

He confirms with a tight nod. "The only family my mom had

were her parents. They had her late in life and didn't have the means to take us in, not that she would ask. Mom refused to move back to Vegas. I was established in school and she didn't want to disrupt my life more than it already had been. A part of me knew she was holding out hope my father would one day change his mind and come back to us. Even with all the bullshit he had put her through, she was still in love with him." His scowl deepens and his jaw tightens. "My mother worked her fingers to the bone with two jobs to keep me in the private school I had been in since kindergarten because she wanted me to have the best education. The commute from our shitty neighborhood to school was an hour twice a day. Not once did my mom complain. Even when I became a rebellious teenager, and started acting out and being an all-around shit; she still never complained. I was your typical mad at the world kid. I was skipping school and getting into fights. The final stunt that landed me in hot water was the time I skipped school and took the train to the city. I snuck into the parking garage where my father worked and vandalized his car. A car he paid one hundred grand for yet didn't pay my mom a dime for in child support. All because he was the rich and powerful Thomas Rowley. He had an endless amount of cash at his disposal and my mom couldn't afford a lawyer."

"What did your father do for work?"

"He owned a media company."

"I read online you inherited all his assets?"

"I did. At first, I didn't want anything to do with his money. My father had reached out to me a month before he passed. He wanted to make amends. I refused to see him. I washed my hands of my father when I was ten. I was pissed when I found out he'd left me everything in his will. His company, his money, his house; all of it."

"What did you do?"

"In the end, I took it. I sold off his company and his possessions. I had no desire or use for any of it. The money allows me to do all the pro bono cases I take on."

I sit and ponder what Callan has told me. "So, what happened after you vandalized your dad's car?"

"I was arrested and sent to juvenile detention. The whole incident was caught on camera. My father didn't hesitate to press charges."

"How long were you in detention?"

"A week. That was how I met Judge Marshall, Frances's husband."

"Frances did mention she has known you for years." I smile.

"It was Richard who saved me from continuing my downward spiral. He didn't look at me like I was just another troubled teen. He saw a boy desperate for help; for guidance. He ended up giving me community service working for him. It was years later I asked him what made him choose to help me. He said that after reading my case, he called my mother. They ended up having a lengthy conversation about our situation and the lack of relationship I had with my father. Richard said it was his heart that led him to make the ruling. I served my community service alongside him. It was then Richard became my mentor. He has been like a father to me ever since. And Frances is like a second mom."

"I'm glad you have that with Frances and Richard. You're lucky to have had an amazing mom. What was her name? I don't believe you've mentioned it."

"Kathleen Hawk."

I think back to the initials on Callan's tattoo. "The letters scribed below your hawk tattoo; are they for your mom?"

Callan nods. "I got the hawks as soon as I was old enough to get inked. To remind myself that no matter what, my mom and I always have each other."

"That's beautiful, Callan."

Callan gets a faraway look on his face. "You know, Richard did the same for Spencer. That's how we met. His story is a lot different than mine, but he too was a troubled young man that Richard saw potential in. The two of us have been friends since we were sixteen."

I laugh. "I have a feeling that Spencer is still trouble, but in a different way. Especially with the ladies."

Callan levels me with an irritated look. "What do you mean by that?"

I roll my eyes. "Calm down, caveman. I mean he's a terrible flirt."

"Yeah, well, the next time he tries that shit with you, he's going to get his ass kicked."

"Oh, please. Spencer likes to push your buttons. Besides, I think he's sweet." Calling Callan's best friend sweet was the wrong thing to do, because, in a flash, Callan is on me, my back pinned to the bed.

"Care to repeat that, baby?" He smiles down at me.

A giggle escapes my mouth. "No."

"I didn't think so." Callan's mouth crashes down on mine.

Wrapping my arms around his neck, he settles his weight between my legs, and I sigh into his mouth. Callan reaches between us and slides his hand past the waistband of my panties, and grabs hold of my butt. My pussy clenches as the rigid length of his erection pressed against my center.

Without hesitation, I reach down and begin pulling at the boxer briefs separating us, and keep my eyes on Callan's the whole time, silently communicating I'm ready to become his in every sense of the word.

"You sure, baby?"

"Yes, Callan. I'm sure."

Sitting back on his haunches, Callan hooks his fingers into the sides of my panties, pulling them from my body the same time I rid myself of my sleep shirt. Leaving me completely exposed.

Callan runs his finger through the seam of my pussy. "I'm going to get you ready for me."

Cupping my butt in his hands, Callan brings his mouth to my pussy. He takes a slow, swipe at my center, licking me from bottom to top. A moan escapes past my lips when he takes my clit into his hot mouth and sucks. There's something erotic in how he not once breaks eye contact. When he pushes in with those long digits of his, hitting that magical spot, while his tongue continues to flick over my clit, my walls start to flutter. I protest when he breaks our connection and my impending orgasm fades. I whimper. "Callan."

"Shh, Baby." Callan settles his weight over the top of my body. This time when he kisses me, I taste myself on his lips. When the head of his cock nudges at my opening, my hips thrust forward, taking him in an inch. With just the head being a tight fit, I momentarily wonder how the rest of him will follow.

"Relax for me, Denver. Open up and let me in."

Thrusting forward, Callan sinks in another inch before pulling out. He repeats the move several more times. It doesn't take long before his length is drenched with my arousal, making me a needy bundle of nerves. As soon as Callan knows I'm relaxed enough, he thrusts forward, breaking through that final barrier, making me his entirely. My nails dig into his back as I cry out his name.

Callan rests his forehead against mine and lets out a curse. "Fuck." The pain isn't too bad. It's more getting used to the feeling of being so full. "Baby. You okay?" I flex my hips, giving him my answer, and causing Callan to hiss. "Fuck. You keep moving and I'm going to come before I'm ready." He kisses me. His tongue delves into my mouth, tasting me for several seconds. A moan escapes my mouth when he starts to move again. "So, fucking tight." Callan moves at a torturous pace. His cock glides in and out of me with slow, long strokes. Leaning down, he takes one of my nipples into his mouth, and I pant.

"Oh, God."

"Come for me, Denver. I want to feel you come all over my cock." When Callan snakes his hand between our joined bodies and uses the pad of his thumb to strum my clit, I explode. My orgasm crashes through me as my walls clamp down around his length, sending him with me. With one final push, he stills, the head of his cock swelling as he spills his release inside me.

Breathing heavy, Callan kisses my shoulder, up my neck, and finally my lips. "You're mine," he states, his eyes searching mine as he hovers above me.

I brush my lips softly against his, a mere breath away from saying what my heart is singing. "I'm yours."

That night, after an invite, Callan and I arrive at Frances and her husband Richard's house for dinner. They live in a two-story brownstone. Greeting us at the door is Frances. She gives me her usual warm smile, making me feel welcome. "Come in you two. Hang your coats and follow me into the living room. Richard had a phone call to make but will be down in a minute."

Callan helps me with my coat then hangs his and mine on a hook by the front door. "Smells good in here, Frances."

"Oh, you know I have to make your favorite when you come over." Frances swats at Callan's arm before turning to me. "Callan loves my homemade lasagna. I don't make it often on account of Richards cholesterol."

"Yeah. My wife is a real hardass when it comes to my diet. I look at it as she wants me to stick around on this earth a while longer." A tall man with grey hair, kind blue eyes and an impressive handlebar mustache strides up behind Frances and kisses her cheek. "I think she likes me." He waggles his brows, being playful with his wife. Frances giggles like a schoolgirl, and I find it endearing.

"Richard, stop being a mess long enough to meet our guest. This is Denver," Frances introduces me.

The older gentleman regards me. The top lip under his bushy

mustache turns up in a knowing smile. "So, this is Callan's Denver."

"Oh, Jesus," Callan mutters.

I hold my hand out. "It's nice to meet you, Sir."

"None of that sir stuff. You can call me Richard." Richard turns his attention to Callan. "Son. Good to see you. Though it's been a while."

"Yeah. I just wrapped up a case, and I have court again Monday morning."

"I heard you handed Dennis his ass and the judge awarded his wife a pretty hefty settlement. Serves the son of a bitch right. I met him at a charity dinner some years back. He is one sour bastard."

Callan chuckles. "Yeah. Well, he's even more so now that he's paying his wife half of everything he's worth."

"Enough talking shop, boys. Let's go eat." Frances ushers us into the dining room.

Just as we are about to sit down at the table, the doorbell chimes, and Frances excuses herself. "That must be Spencer. He said he might stop by."

A second later, Frances returns with Spencer in tow. "I know you all didn't start without me. What's for dinner?" Spencer's eyes cut around the table, landing on me. "Well, well. Hey there, sweetheart."

I give him a little wave. "Hi Spencer. How are you?"

"Better now that I've seen your pretty face."

Callan jumps in. "Unless you're looking to end your night in the emergency room, I suggest you shut the hell up."

"Boys. Play nice, and Callan, watch your language," Frances scolds.

"Frances. How come you don't get on to the old man for cursing but ride mine and Callan's tails about it?" Spencer asks.

"It's because I'm old and set in my ways. She thinks you two are still young enough to be taught better," Richard answers.

The remainder of dinner is spent listening to Richard tell stories about Callan and Spencer, and some of the mischief they got into. For once in my life I feel what it's like to be around a family who genuinely cares for one another.

As we're putting our coats on and getting ready to leave, Frances stops us. "I almost forgot. When I left work early Friday, I left the Branson file on my desk. Kelly was nice enough to bring it to me. I knew you would need them first thing Monday morning since you are going straight to court and not the office." She hands the file to Callan.

"Thanks, Frances." He kisses her cheek then shakes Richard's hand.

The four of us say our goodbyes before Callan, and I take our leave.

14

DENVER

When Monday morning sneaks up on me, I wake before the alarm sounds. Wiping the sleep from my eyes, I stretch and peer at the clock on the table beside the bed. Knowing I won't be able to go back to sleep, I slid out from under the blanket, careful not to disturb Callan.

Standing at the foot of the bed, I study the man sleeping in front of me, taking in his relaxed features, two-day-old stubble on his face, and his tousled hair. I'm not sure if a man would like to be described as beautiful, but Callan is. He's also caring and passionate once you get passed his asshole exterior. The smile on my face grows as I stare at him a tad longer.

"I feel your eyes on me," Callan says, his voice gruff from sleep, then opens his to slits. "What are you doing out of bed?"

"Couldn't sleep any longer, so I'm about to take a shower. You can go back to sleep."

Callan tosses the blanket to the side and climbs out of bed. "I'll join you."

My belly dips, and I don't miss the evil glint in his eyes before turning on my heel, and ambling into the bathroom with him behind me. Callan makes his intentions known when he opens a drawer below the bathroom counter, retrieving a box of condoms.

My heart rate increases, and I bite my lower lip to suppress my smile.

After Callan and I had sex for the first time yesterday morning, I mentioned the fact I've only been on the pill a week, and it wasn't effective yet. I also noted I was due for my period soon and due to timing, we were probably in the clear.

Reaching into the shower, I turn on the hot water while Callan steps out of his boxer briefs then effectively rids me of my t-shirt and panties. I go about shampooing my hair while Callan takes the body wash, squeezes some out into the palm of his hand, then rubs them together, working up a good lather. He starts by running his hands from my neck, down the valley between my breasts, across my stomach, before snaking his hands around to my backside, caressing the curves of my ass. He palms my cheeks, then reaches between my legs, slightly touching my already sensitive clit. His finger teases my pussy, finding it already wet. "You sore?" "A little," I say, my voice heavy with desire.

Dipping his head, Callan peppers kisses along my shoulder and neck, causing my entire body to shiver, my nipples to harden, and leaving my breasts feeling heavy from his teasing. "Come here." Callan hoists me up, and I wrap my legs around his waist as he walks us backward, then sits on the tiled bench at the far end of his massive shower. "So sweet. So, fucking sexy," he says between kisses as he palms the cheeks of my ass once more.

Reaching for the condom he'd placed on the shower shelf, Callan puts the foil wrapper between his teeth, and rips it open. I watch as he reaches between our bodies and sheaths his cock. "Ride me," he orders, and without hesitation, I do as he commands.

Rising to my knees, I rest my hands on his shoulders while he guides the blunt head of his cock to my entrance. With Callan's hands clasped at my waist, I take a deep breath, and slowly lower myself until his cock is buried inside me, completely. Today, there is no pain, only the feeling of being full. Callan releases a strangled grunt as I begin to rock my hips, getting used to the new sensation.

"I like it like this," I tell him as I grind down harder.

"Fuck," he hisses, tightening his grip on my hips.

Callan's face looks as if he's in pain, and I stop moving. My heart drops with the notion I'm doing this the wrong way. I'm sure he is used to women with more experience. "Am I doing it wrong?" Callan's features change as he cups my face in his hands. "Everything you do is perfect. I want you to move the way your body is telling you to. I promise there is no greater feeling in the world than being inside you, Denver. My problem is you feel too good. I'm seconds away from blowing, and I'm not ready yet."

At his confession, I relax and do as he says. I move my body in whatever way makes it feel good while Callan palms my breasts. The moment he takes one of my nipples into his mouth, I throw my head back. "Callan."

"That's it, baby. Take what's yours."

Soon, the pleasure becomes too much, and Callan decides to take over. Standing from the bench, our connection is broken as he turns, and suddenly my back is pressed against the cold tile of the shower wall. With no time to think about the agonizing empty feeling between my legs, Callan remedies it by slamming back into me in one fluid motion, causing me to gasp. Our mouths meet in an urgent kiss. With our bodies pressed against one another, I feel the rapid beat of his heart. "Jesus." Callan pulls out then surges back in. I push my hips down, trying to match his rhythm.

"You feel so good inside me," I moan, gripping his shoulders. Sooner than I'd like, my belly tightens, and the walls of my pussy begin to flutter.

"Shit, baby, I'm coming." Callan works himself in and out of me at a rapid pace. "Come with me."

My body working in rhythm with his, I throw my head back, and my lips part. "Oh, god!" My orgasm surges through my entire body.

With one final thrust, Callan falls with me, and I pull him in tighter as we ride out our release together.

A short hour later, before work, Callan takes me to a hole-in-the-wall diner where the woman behind the counter calls him by name, and where they serve the best French Toast in the city. His words, not mine. As we sit getting ready to eat our meal, I start to hum along to the Christmas music playing in the background, and a thought comes to mind. "Do you have any plans for Christmas?" I take another bite of my French Toast, enjoying the robust cinnamon flavor.

"I usually stay at home. On Christmas Eve Spencer and I eat dinner with Frances and Richard, but normally my Christmas day is spent alone." Callan downs his coffee. "However, I have thought about taking a trip this year." His eyes gleam when he looks at me, cocking his head. "Why?"

Shrugging, I take a small sip of my caramel latte. "No reason. I thought we could maybe get a small tree for the Penthouse. I've never had my own tree before. I thought it would be fun." Sitting my mug on the table, I wave my hand. "It was a silly idea. Forget I said anything."

Callan pauses before placing another bite of food into his mouth. "Nonsense. You want to get a tree and decorate it; we will. I'll buy you the biggest fucking tree we can find if that's what will make you happy."

"Really?" I can't contain my excitement as I bounce in my seat.

Callan chuckles, then leans over the table, kissing me. "Really, baby. We'll go today after work and pick one out."

Sitting at my desk a couple of hours later, I rub my temples, trying to soothe the throbbing in my head. We're only a few hours into the workday, and already, Callan is in a sour mood. He received a phone call soon after arriving at the office, and whoever it was set him off. Now he's snapping people's heads off left and right. "Miss Hollis!" Callan's irritated voice barks over the intercom from the phone sitting on top of my desk "Is the boardroom set up for my three o'clock?"

"No. I was..."

He cuts me off. "Get it done."

Gritting my teeth, I resist the urge to walk into his office and strangle him. I was on my way to do just that, but once again, I didn't have the opportunity to tell him so, before he barked at me. Instead, I give Callan my best sweet voice. "Yes, Mr. Hawk. I'm right on top of that...asshole," I must not have released the intercom button in time because his voice fills the air once again.

This time sounding more amused than angry.

"I heard that, Miss Hollis."

After I take care of making sure we have enough bottled water, and place a call to our usual catering company for Callan's meeting, I sit back down at my desk and find several new emails. One of them from Spencer. The subject line reads PLUS ONE CONFIRMATION. I open the email.

Mr. Hawk, please confirm a plus one to tonight's dinner.
Beverly.

Beverly is Spencer's PA of the week. Apparently, his assistant is on maternity leave and for the last month he hasn't been able to hold onto a temp longer than a day or two. Let's see how long Beverly lasts. Pulling up Callan's schedule for today, I don't see anything regarding dinner tonight. Crap. Now I have to go into the lion's den and ask Mr. Grumpy about it. Blowing out a breath, I push away from my desk, make my way to Callan's office door and knock.

"What?"

I step into his office. "I received an email from Beverly."

Callan looks up from his computer. "Okay. Who is Beverly?"

"Beverly is Spencer's assistant and she would like to confirm whether or not you will be bringing a plus one to the dinner tonight?"

Callan scrunches his brow in confusion for a second before cursing, "Shit."

"I'm sorry. I checked your schedule and didn't see anything about dinner. I would have reminded you if I had."

He runs his hand down his face. "It's not your fault, baby. My last assistant must not have added it to my schedule when the invitations were sent out months ago." Callan picks up the phone on his desk and punches some numbers. "Hey, Frances. I need you to reschedule my three o'clock." He looks up from the papers lying in front of him, and smiles at me. "Yeah, everything is alright. I just remembered Spencer's dinner thing is tonight. I'm taking Denver on an extended lunch." Callan's smile grows, making me smile too. "Will do." Standing, Callan strides over to where his suit jacket hangs and puts it on. "Grab your purse. We have shopping to do."

"What are you talking about?" I trail behind him and grab my purse from my desk drawer as he waits for me.

"You're going with me to Spencer's charity dinner tonight. You'll need a dress."

A short time later, Callan and I arrive at a department store where his personal stylist greets us. "Mr. Hawk, Miss Hollis. It's good to see you."

"Maggie, it's good to see you again." Callan pulls me to his side. "I'd like you to meet my girlfriend, Denver."

I offer my hand. "It's nice to meet you."

"It's good to finally put a face to the woman I've had the pleasure of shopping for. And now that I see all this gorgeous red hair," she gestures, "I can't wait to pick you out some more appropriate pieces to accentuate all your fabulous features." Pivoting on her heel, she crosses the room. "I have the perfect gown for you."

Maggie leads Callan and me to a more secluded part of the store. Callan takes a seat on the chair and gives me a panty-melting smile as Maggie leads me to a large changing room. The moment she pulls back the curtain I gasp. Hanging in front of me is the most beautiful dress I have ever laid eyes on. "I can't wait to see this dress on you, Denver. I know it's going to be stunning." Maggie beams, clasping her hands together.

After stripping down to my bra and panties, she helps me into the gown. Once the back of the dress is zipped, I take a deep breath, and face the floor-length mirror. My breath catches as I take in my reflection.

"Perfect," Maggie whispers her approval. The velvet, long sleeve emerald green gown hugs my curves perfectly. I stare at my reflection, thinking how could the beautiful woman looking back, be me. I run my palms over the luxurious fabric. The deep v-neck, which shows off a bit of cleavage, plummets to my torso, where a belt cinches my waist in, accentuating the slight flare of my hips. The long slit up the right side stops about mid-thigh, showing the perfect amount of leg, making the gown sexy, yet tasteful. I feel like a princess. "I have never worn something this beautiful."

"Oh, honey. The dress is beautiful, but you make it look like a piece of art." Turning Maggie opens a box sitting on the tufted bench, pulling out a pair of matching green, five-inch strappy heels. "Let's get these on you." Crouching down to the floor, she helps me slip the shoes on. "Let's show Mr. Hawk." Maggie pulls back the curtain, and I step through. I walk into the waiting area, where Callan is sitting. He looks up from his phone. His nostrils flare as his eyes travel the length of my body.

"What do you think?" I ask nervously, and try not to fidget.

Without taking his focus off me, he says, "We'll take it—shoes too. Please have it delivered to my Penthouse by four." He hands Maggie his credit card.

Hours later, I'm riding in the back of a limo next to Callan with my nerves all over the place. I've never been to a fancy function before. "What charity is this event for?"

"Domestic violence. Spencer started holding charity dinners eight years ago. Once he started making a name for himself, he took advantage of his platform and connections. He's not big on rubbing elbows with most of the people in attendance, but the money and donations the event brings are well worth it."

"I think what he's doing is admirable. There are not enough people in the world like you and Spencer. You two use your money and power to make a difference."

Callan threads his hand with mine, bringing it to his lips. "Most people who attend don't come from humble beginnings like Spencer and me. They don't know those kinds of struggles. Unfortunately, a majority of them only donate because it makes them look good on paper."

"That's horrible."

"It is," Callan agrees. "But, at the end of the day, his goal is getting inside their pockets and helping those who are less fortunate." The limo stops in front of one of New York's most famous hotels. A red carpet paves the way to the entrance, and lining the rug is a slew of photographers. Callan turns to me. "You ready, baby?"

"You didn't tell me the press would be here."

"Because I knew you'd be nervous." He grins. "Come on." Callan steps out of the limo when the driver opens the door.

The cameras start flashing and people begin shouting, "Mr. Hawk, over here!"

This is insane. How has this become my life? I feel like a fish out of water—an imposter. Calming my nerves, I take a deep breath. Taking the hand Callan has held out for me and allow him to help me from the car.

"Who's your date, Mr. Hawk?" another photographer shouts.

Keeping my hand in his, we ignore the flashing lights and photographers as Callan leads us inside. According to my google search weeks ago, I knew Callan was a big deal and very well known, but I wasn't at all prepared for this. "That was a bit overwhelming. Do you ever get used to it?"

"Unfortunately, yes. But they're not as bad as they were right after my father passed away and I sold his company. At one point it was a struggle leaving my home at all. Now, they mostly show up at events like this one to catch a glimpse of who's showing up with who. The gossip rags don't care about tonight's cause. They only care about getting their money shot, and the hopes one of tonight's A-listers will get drunk and show out."

"Does that sort of thing happen at these kinds of events?"

"Celebrities getting wasted?" Callan shrugs. "Sometimes. It's never happened at one of Spencer's events. He runs a tight ship and has staff on hand to handle anything, or anyone that may get out of hand. He won't allow any bad press to taint his work. Spencer takes what he does very seriously."

Walking hand in hand into the grand ballroom, my eyes scan the massive space lit in a romantic amber glow, and begin to feel overwhelmed as I take in at least two hundred guests in attendance.

"Relax, baby," Callan whispers into my ear.

"I feel so out of place. Like a fraud amongst all these elegant and posh people."

Callan lets go of my hand and snakes his arm around my waist. "Don't let their faces fool you. None of them are half as good as you are. You're more authentic than they will ever be." Callan presses his lips to my temple. "You're by my side, exactly where I want you to be and where you belong." Callan gazes down at me.

The truth in his words shows on his face. "Come on. Let's get some champagne."

Keeping to the edge of the crowd, we make our way to the bar, where Callan orders two drinks. "One champagne and a glass of scotch, please."

"Callan, Denver. I'm glad the two of you could make it." At the sound of Spencer's voice, both Callan and I turn. The smile on my face diminishes the instant I notice who is on his arm. Kelly is pressed against Spencer, wearing a short black satin number, that has more of a night club vibe than an upscale charity feel. She gives me her usual bitch face, and I avoid looking at her, trying to pretend she doesn't exist. I'm shocked to see her here with Spencer. I thought she was after Callan. Then again, Kelly is probably an opportunist who will latch on to whoever will give her the time of day. "Denver," Spencer calls my name, drawing my attention. "You look fucking radiant." He breaks away from Kelly and kisses my cheek.

I smile. "Thanks, Spencer."

Spencer gives me a wink, his action pissing off his date. "You are one lucky son of a bitch, Callan." He slaps his friend on the shoulder, and Callan pulls me into his side.

"I know. Now, if you don't mind, would you stop eye-fucking my woman?"

Spencer throws his head back and laughs, clearly getting a kick out of messing with his friend. Kelly, however, is not as amused.

"Spencer, darling. I want a drink." Kelly tugs on Spencer's arm to gain his attention.

His smile disappears as he turns toward her, speaking in a clipped tone. "Why don't you head on over to the bar and wait for me?"

Huffing, Kelly pinches her lips together, and cuts her eyes at me, before scuttling off in the direction of the bar. My dislike for the woman must be showing all over my face because Spencer chuckles. "Not a fan of my date?"

"You could do better," I mutter under my breath without thinking. Luckily Spencer doesn't take offense.

"Thought you had cut Kelly loose weeks ago?" Callan asks his best friend.

Spencer sighs. "Yeah, me too." He rubs the back of his neck. "Her ass showed up tonight. I would have tossed her out but didn't want to cause a scene."

The sound of Kelly's giggle from across the room draws our attention. The three of us look toward the bar to see her leaning over the counter while chatting with the bartender, her boobs on the verge of popping out. Spencer signals for a man standing by the front entrance, and faces us. "Let me go take care of her. I'll catch you two later."

Throughout the night, Callan introduces me to multiple contributors, some of whom were very pleasant. Now, sitting at the table, along with Spencer, Frances, and her Richard; all my worries, and nervousness are all but forgotten, as we laugh and enjoy the delicious food served a short time ago. Placing my napkin on the table, I lean into Callan. "I'm going to the ladies' room before Spencer makes his speech."

"You want me to go with you?"

I shake my head, laughing. "I can make my own way. You stay and finish your meal."

"Would you like another champagne?"

Pushing my chair from the table, I stand with my clutch in hand. "No, thank you. I think I've had enough. Maybe just water." I smile down at Callan, his stare giving me butterflies in my stomach.

"You got it, baby."

I lean down and plant a soft kiss on his lips. "I'll be right back."

As I enter the bathroom, two women are reapplying their

lipstick. We exchange polite smiles before I step into one of the stalls. When I exit the stall, I'm surprised to find Kelly standing there. It was my understanding Spencer had her escorted out of the building. "Looks like Callan was able to clean up the gutter trash," she says with disdain. I cock my head to the side. I still haven't figured out Kelly's angle. At first, I thought she was trying to gain Callan's attention, then she shows up tonight on Spencer's arm. Now she is back to snide comments and nasty stares.

"You know, Kelly. You're wasting your breath. I have no intention of playing these childish games with you. I don't know what your goal is here but I'm with Callan. I'm living in his apartment and sleeping in his bed every night. Get over it."

Kelly saunters up to me, getting in my face. "Soon, Callan will see you for what you are, and you'll be back to sleeping next to the dumpster where you belong." Bumping into my shoulder as she passes by, Kelly disappears out of the bathroom door. Usually, her threats don't affect me, but for some reason, this time feels different. Her words leave an uneasy feeling in the pit of my stomach.

I run into Callan as I exit the bathroom. "I was coming to look for you." Callan looks at me with concern. "Everything okay, baby?"

Masking my worries from my encounter with Kelly, I smile. "Of course."

"You sure?"

"I'm sure." I link my arm with his. "Come on. We don't want to miss Spencer's speech."

15

DENVER

The following day, I push aside Kelly's warning, and decided not to let her jealousy ruin my happiness. It's nearly time to call it a day, when I come upon Lucas' office and knock on the open door.

Lucas is standing at his desk with his back to me. "Hey. Lucas." He turns. "Hey, Denver. What brings you by?"

"I tried your extension, but you didn't answer. Mr. Hawk is on his way back to the office and wants to see you before you go home for the day."

"No problem. Thanks for telling me." I turn to leave when Lucas stops me. "Hey, Denver."

"Yeah?"

"My family is throwing my grandfather a party for his sixty ninth birthday. Since he has asked about you a few times, I want to extend an invite. I think he'd be thrilled to see you."

I smile warmly at the thought of his grandfather. "I would love to. I've meant to go by the library to see him. It's because of him I got this job." Lucas probably knows about my previous situation from his grandfather and I am grateful he has never brought it up.

"Great." Lucas reaches into his briefcase and pulls out an envelope, handing it to me. "All the details are on the invitation. Feel free to bring a friend." He gives me a knowing wink.

"Thanks, Lucas I just might do that."

Lucas peers down at his watch. "I bet the boss is back by now. How about I walk with you?"

"Sure." As Lucas and I make our way back to my end of the office, a commotion can be heard, and I make out Kelly and Frances arguing. Lucas and I give each other a confused look. "What in the world is going on?" My steps quicken as Kelly's voice raises an octave. When we reach the two arguing women they are standing at my desk. "Frances, is everything okay?"

Kelly is the one to answer. "No, everything is not okay, you little thief." Her evil glare cuts right through me.

My head rears back. "Excuse me?"

Frances places her arms out in front of her to calm Kelly's rant. "Now, Kelly. You need to calm down."

"I will not calm now!" she screeches, swatting France's hands away. "I'm calling the police."

"The police?" I direct my attention back to Kelly. "What for?"

"Yes, the police. My wallet has gone missing, and I know who has it."

"Who?" I ask.

Kelly looks me dead in the face and points her finger at me. "You. You stole my wallet, you fucking thief, and I'm having you arrested."

My stomach drops, and my heart threatens to beat out of my chest. "I didn't take your wallet."

"Whoa, whoa, whoa. Everybody calm down," Lucas interjects, putting himself between a theatrical Kelly and me.

My eyes bounce back and forth between Lucas and Frances. "I swear I didn't take her wallet. I don't know what she's talking about." The unwanted attention sends panic coursing through my body, and I begin to shake. What the hell is going on?

"Oh, please. You think you have everyone here fooled but not me."

"I'm not trying to fool anyone, Kelly. I promise I didn't steal your wallet." I try pleading with her, but my words are falling on deaf ears because she's already on her phone with the police spouting off the address.

"Kelly. You can't go around accusing people of such things and calling the police without proof." Frances takes a step toward Kelly; her expression one of anger. "Denver would do no such thing."

"I agree with Frances," Lucas adds. "Denver is not a thief."

"You two are fools. You'll see once the police get here." Kelly lifts her nose in the air, with a smug look on her face.

"What the hell is going on here!" Callan's voice booms as he barrels down the hall, taking in the current scene. At this point, I am no longer able to hold back the tears. Callan takes me in his arms when he sees the state I'm in.

"Kelly accused Denver of stealing her wallet and has called the police," Frances fills him in.

Callan spins, facing Kelly. "Want to fucking explain?"

Just then, two officers are being escorted toward us by the security guard. "We received a call about a stolen wallet?"

Kelly raises her hand. "Yes, officer. I reported the stolen wallet, and I have reason to believe it was Denver Hollis who took it. I want her belongings searched."

"Now hold on a goddamn minute!" Callan shouts, still holding my shaking body against his.

One of the officers steps forward. "I'm sorry, Sir. But we have to investigate the allegation. Who is Denver Hollis?"

I look up at Callan, then address the officer. "I am," my voice cracks as anxiety tries to strangle me.

The officer then addresses me. "Ma'am. I'm going to need to search your belongings."

"She doesn't have to do shit," Callan spits, trying to interject once again.

I place my hand on his arm. "Let them do their job, Callan. I didn't take anything." He gives me a tight nod. Stepping out of his hold, I walk to my desk and retrieve my purse. "Here you go, officer."

The cop takes my purse and proceeds to dump its contents out on top of the desk in front of everyone. The first thing to land on top of my desk is an unrecognizable Chanel wallet. My mouth opens in shock.

"You see!" Kelly yells, pointing at the pile of stuff laid out on the desk. "I knew she stole it."

I now have six sets of eyes on me. "I don't know how that got in there, I swear," I plead with tears running down my face.

The officer then picks up a scarf, and when he does, a necklace falls out. He picks it up. "Is this your necklace, Ma'am?"

I eye the jewelry. "No. I've never seen that before in my life. I don't know why it was in my bag."

Frances is the next to speak up. "That necklace belongs to me." Her tone is low with shock. "It was my mother's." She looks at the jewelry in the cop's hand, then to me. Her brow scrunches with confusion.

"Frances, I swear I didn't take it. I would never do something like that."

"Just like when you started working here, you didn't steal food from the faculty lounge?" Kelly accuses, her tone sarcastic.

"I..." my eyes dart around the room as people scrutinize me with their stares. "That was different," I say in an ashamed whisper. I look to Callan, who has suddenly gone silent. He's looking at me like I'm a stranger. Does he honestly believe what I'm accused of ? "Callan?" I reach for him only to have him take a step back. My heart plummets to the floor. "Callan. You don't believe I did this, do you? I would never..."

Callan looks at me with hurt and betrayal. "Then why were those items, not belonging to you, in your bag, Denver? Did you take that necklace when we were at Frances's the other night for dinner?"

"No!" I sob. "I didn't do this." I turn to Frances. "I didn't take your necklace, Frances."

Frances still carries a look of confusion, and just as she's about to open her mouth, the officer speaks. "I'm sorry, but you're going to have to come with us, Miss Hollis." The cop takes the handcuffs from his belt and steps to me. "I have to place you under arrest. Do you understand?"

I look to Callan and plead once again. "Callan, please. Don't let them arrest me. I didn't do it. Please," I cry, and Callan grinds his jaw. Turning his face away, he refuses to look at me. I cut my eyes to Frances then to Lucas. Both look on with pity. Kelly, however, looks like she's just won.

Taking my wrists in his hands, the cop slaps the handcuffs on me while reading me my rights. As the police lead me down the hall, I'm in hysterics as I look back. "Callan, please!" I shout, terrified, and hurt. The whole time they escort me from the building, I expect Callan to fight for me, but that moment never happens. As I'm placed in the back of the police cruiser, I realize the man I am in love with, and the man I thought cared about me, doesn't believe in me. It feels as if the entire universe has caved in, crushing my soul in the process.

Fifteen minutes later, I'm being fingerprinted, and my picture taken. "Do you have anyone you want to call?" the officer asks.

Wrapping my arms around my body, I shake my head. "I don't have anybody."

Next, I'm led into a room with a table and two chairs where the police officer proceeds to question me for over an hour. He asks me the same questions over and over as if my answers will suddenly change. Only they don't. I didn't take the wallet or the necklace, and I have no clue as to how they ended up in my purse.

None of it matters. It doesn't matter what I say. The evidence is damning. Hell, even I can admit I look guilty.

After questioning, the officer shows me to my cell, then sighs. "Alright. You'll have to hang tight here until a judge can see you. That won't be until sometime tomorrow or the next day. Are you sure you don't have someone you'd like to call?"

Sitting on the concrete bench, I look around, and take in my sleeping arrangements for the night. "Like I told you before, officer. I don't have anyone." A cold draft causes me to shiver, as he closes the heavy steel door.

I honestly have no one.

THE NEXT MORNING, I'm startled by the opening of the cell door. "Let's go, Hollis. You made bail, and your attorney is waiting for you in the lobby."

I sit up. "My attorney?" My first thought is of Callan as I rub the ache from my eyes.

"Your attorney, Mr. Knight. Now let's go."

What is Spencer doing here? I follow the officer down the hall, to the front of the police station, where I'm met by Callan's best friend Spencer, who's face morphs into a murderous expression when he gets a glimpse at my current state. I'm in yesterday's clothes which doesn't bother me, but I'm sure my red puffy face, mascara that is probably smudged all over the place and my messy hair situation don't make me look any better.

"Ma'am." A woman sitting behind the counter, with plexiglass separating us stops me. "I have your belongings." She pulls my purse out of a bag marked evidence.

I take the bag from her; the one Callan gave to me as a gift and reach inside for my wallet. Opening it, I take what cash I have, my phone, and my ID, then stuff both into my pocket. Once I have what I need, I look back at the woman. "Do you have a trash can back there?"

She lifts a brow. "Yes."

I slide the purse across the counter. "Will you toss this in there? I don't need it."

"Are you sure? That bag is worth thousands." She appears shocked.

"It's not worth a damn thing to me," I tell her, walking away.

Avoiding eye contact with Spencer, I head toward the exit door. "What are you doing here, Spencer?" Grabbing my arm, he stops me. Turning my body to face his, Spencer places his finger under my chin, lifting it. "I came to do what my asshole best friend should have, and that is to get you out of here."

My bottom lip wobbles. "You don't believe I did it?"

"Fuck no. And neither does Frances. She's the one who called me yesterday. I was out of town and didn't get back until late. I'm so fucking sorry I didn't get here sooner, Denver."

"Frances believes me too?" My voice rises slightly, causing a couple of people in the lobby to stare.

"Hell, yeah. We know you didn't take shit."

"What happens now?" I divert my eyes.

"You let me do my job."

I nod. "Thanks for getting me out of here. I promise to pay you back somehow."

"Fuck that. You're not paying me back, Denver."

Licking my dry lips, I look around as I try to think about my next move. There is no way I can go to Callan's. He hates me and thinks I'm a criminal. I have some cash I've been saving since living with Callan, but not much. It suddenly dawns on me; not only do I not have a place to live, but I am also out of a job. I'm back to where I was weeks ago. At this point, I'm too exhausted to think. What I need is a shower and some time to wrap my head around what's happened. "Do you think you can give me a ride to a hotel? Someplace cheap?" I ask Spencer.

His lips thin. "I have been given strict instructions to take you elsewhere."

"Where are you supposed to take me?"

"Come on. You'll see." Too tired to argue, I follow Spencer. The fact he showed to bail me out, and knowing he believes my innocence makes my decision to trust him much easier.

Fifteen minutes later, we pull up in front of Frances's home. I look at Spencer, who is sitting in the driver's seat. "Frances insisted. They have been worried sick." I don't get a chance to protest. Quite frankly, I don't want to. Spencer climbs out, and walks around his car, then opens my door. By the time I step out, Frances and her husband are waiting at their front door, worry etched on their faces.

Frances pulls me in for a tight hug. "Oh, dear. I'm so sorry this happened." She then ushers me inside with Spencer following behind. "Let's get you warmed up. How about some coffee, and breakfast?"

"Just some coffee is fine. I'm not hungry," I tell her.

"Let's all go sit at the kitchen table. Richard and I have something we'd like to discuss with the two of you," Frances says, looking between Spencer and me.

"Do you mind if I use your bathroom first?"

"Go right ahead." Frances gives me a warm smile, her eyes looking tired.

Stepping into the bathroom, I brace my palms against the sink and take three deep breaths. My nose starts to sting as tears threaten to fall, and I try with all I have to hold them back but fail. Stumbling backward, my legs give out and I slide down against the wall, falling to my bottom beside the tub. I don't know how long I sit propped up against the cold bathtub crying before a soft knock at the door draws my attention. "Denver, are you okay?" Spencer asks. He knocks again when I fail to answer. "I'm coming in." The bathroom door pushes open. "Shit." He drops down to one knee in front of me.

"I don't know how I can get through this, Spencer. Yesterday I woke up in the arms of the man I love, who I thought cared about me, and this morning I woke up in a jail cell—no more Callan. No home. No job." I look up at Spencer. "I don't know where to go from here."

Spencer reaches for a washcloth sitting on the sink, runs hot water over it, then starts wiping my tears and day-old makeup from my face. "I promise everything is going to work out, Denver." Spencer makes a few more passes across my cheeks with the cloth before he tosses it on the counter. "Come on. Up you go." He holds out his hand, and I take it, allowing him to pull me off the cold bathroom floor.

"Anyone ever tell you how sweet you are, Spencer? Instead of taking Callan's side, you're here, with me, wiping the tears and snot from my face." I sniffle.

"Callan is my best friend, but he fucked up this time. I know it. You know it, and someday soon, he'll realize it too. Which I'm willing to bet is going to be sooner rather than later."

"It doesn't matter, Spencer. The damage is done. I don't think I can forgive him." I hiccup. "If you'd seen the way he looked at me yesterday..." I shake my head. "I begged him, Spencer. I begged him to believe me."

Spencer's face softens. "I'm sorry, Denver. But I know Callan, and I'm willing to bet my life he's in love with you." He kisses the top of my head. "Let's go out here and see what Frances and Richard have to say. Okay?"

I nod, and try to fix my hair. "Okay."

Fifteen minutes and one cup of coffee later, I sit stunned at the kitchen table as Frances and Richard tell Spencer and me their theory on how Kelly's wallet and her jewelry found their way inside my purse. "Fuck." Spencer leans back in his chair, crossing his arms over his chest.

I look at Frances. "You believe Kelly planted everything?"

"Oh, I know she did. The scarf the police found my necklace wrapped in belongs to Kelly. When I first saw it, I thought it looked familiar but couldn't place where I had seen it before. It wasn't until an hour after your arrest it dawned on me. She was wearing it the day she brought those files to my house. You remember the night you and Callan came over for dinner?" I give Frances a nod, and she continues. "I had left the office early that day and forgot them. Kelly was all too eager to stop by my house with them. She was wearing that scarf when she arrived."

I shake my head. "Kelly can claim I stole the scarf along with the wallet."

Spencer sits forward, jumping in. "Frances. Did Kelly enter the residence when she dropped by?"

"She did. She asked to use the bathroom."

"Son of a bitch," Spencer hisses.

I look at him. "So, Kelly knew I was going to be here with Callan last Saturday, and you're saying she conveniently offered to bring you the files. When she asked to use the restroom, she swiped the necklace, and planted it in my purse?"

Frances places her hand on her hip. "That's exactly what I'm saying."

"I knew Kelly hated me. She's never been shy about it, or stating she wanted me gone, but to do this? It makes no sense." Yet it does. I lean back in my chair.

"It makes perfect fucking sense. I bet you money Kelly did this shit at the advice of Joslyn."

"Joslyn?" My brow scrunches. "What does Callan's ex have to do with anything?"

"Joslyn and Kelly are friends. They went to college together and are sorority sisters." Spencer stands from the table.

"Where are you going?" I ask.

"I'm going to fix this shit."

I stand too. "Can you still drop me at a hotel?"

"Denver." Frances places a hand on my shoulder, and I turn to face her. "I'd like to offer you a place to stay. We have plenty of room."

"I don't want to put you out. A hotel is fine until I can figure something else out. I'll find another job and..."

Spencer cuts me off. "You can come work for me."

"What?"

"My assistant has gone on maternity leave and informed me the other day she has decided to stay home with her baby indefinitely. You'd be doing me a huge favor."

I think about it for a minute. "Are you sure?"

Spencer grins. "Hell, yeah." He rubs his hands together and smirks. "Not only will you be doing me a favor, but it will also piss off Callan."

I shake my head, "I won't accept the job as a way to punish Callan. That's not what I want."

"You won't be punishing Callan. I know you're too good to do something like that. I, however, am not." Spencer steps up to me. "Can you at least agree to stay with Frances and Richard? Just for a few days and think about my offer?"

I sigh. "Okay. I'll stay and think about it."

"Good." Spencer kisses the top of my head. "Now I'm going to put this bullshit with Kelly to rest. I'll be back later when I have everything taken care of."

As Spencer walks out the door, I send up a silent prayer hoping he can fix my mess. I want to forget any of it ever happened and move on with my life. Even though imagining life without Callan feels like someone is ripping my heart from my chest.

16

CALLAN

I wake with a pounding in my head, and groan. "Fuck." Cracking one eye open, I realize I'm not in my bed. Instead, I'm face down on the living room floor with an empty bottle of Jack sitting next to my face. What the fuck happened last night? Rolling to my back, I stare up at the ceiling as I try to gain some clarity. It doesn't take long for the memories of yesterday's events to come rushing back, and close my eyes, as the vision of Denver's face stricken with fear and hurt flashes through the forefront of my brain. Bile rises in my throat. Picking myself up off the floor, I dash down the hall to the bathroom, lifting the lid of the toilet, where I proceed to empty the contents of my stomach. Shit. How much did I drink?

Stumbling to the sink, I wash my face, brush my teeth, and take in my reflection. "What the fuck are you doing, asshole." Bile threatens to rise in my throat once again when the gravity of my situation punches me in the gut. I've made the worst mistake of my life. Tamping down the urge to retch, I fly out of the bathroom and into the bedroom. Opening the closet door, I grab the first pair of shoes in reach and shove my feet into them. Looking up, my eyes land on the side of the closet filled with Denver's clothes. "Shit!" Denver is probably sitting in a cell right now scared out of her mind, and it's all my fault. Jogging out of the bedroom and down the hall, I stop at the kitchen island long enough to snatch my phone and the keys. The moment I fling the door open, I run into Spencer, standing there with his fist raised.

"Good morning, fuckface." His demeanor hints at his current mood.

"I don't have time for your shit. What do you want, Spencer?"

"Oh? And might I ask where you are rushing off too? It's certainly not to get your woman out of jail where she spent the night. I already took care of that earlier this morning, dumbass." Spencer breezes pass me, bumping my shoulder along the way. "Although," he continues, "I don't think you could call her your girlfriend anymore. Not since you tossed her aside like trash."

My fists clench at my sides. "You want to tell me what you're going on about and where MY woman is?"

"Well, I posted Denver's bail this morning." Spencer walks into my kitchen, opens the refrigerator door, and grabs a protein shake. "And not because you need to know, but because I'm kind of feeling sorry for your hungover ass right now," Spencer opens the drink in his hand, then downs half of it before continuing, "I took her to Frances and Richard's house, because unlike you, the rest of us didn't turn our backs on her." He chucks the empty bottle in the trash can.

Anger has me rushing my best friend. I fist his shirt, getting in his face. "I made a fucking mistake." I push his back against the wall. "Joslyn ambushed me on the sidewalk outside my office yesterday. She started spewing bullshit about how I don't know Denver and how I'm too gullible when it comes to damsels in distress. She fucking got inside my head and put me in a piss mood. Then I walk in on Kelly accusing Denver of stealing. A second later, the police were there, finding not only Kelly's wallet but Frances' necklace in Denver's purse? The evidence was right there." I shake my head. "Then, all the shit Joslyn had said came rushing back. I started doubting mine and Denver's relationship and how quickly I fell for her. For a split second, I wondered if Joslyn was right!" I yell, shoving my friend once more.

Spencer breaks from my hold and pushes me, causing me to stumble back. "You fucked up, and you need to own that shit. You turned your back on Denver. I can't believe you let that bitch Joslyn get in your head. You fought your feelings for Denver since the first day you laid eyes on her, and then, when you finally have her, you pull some shit like this." Spencer stalks away. "Did you even take a minute to hear her out? To get her side of the story? You're a lawyer for Christ's sake, Callan. Yet you tossed her aside as if she were nothing. As if the past few weeks meant jack shit."

"You don't have to tell me this, Spencer. I'm aware of how bad I fucked up." Stepping into my personal space, Spencer levels me with a look I have only seen a handful of times from him.

"I don't think you do know, Callan. You weren't the one who saw the loss of hope in her eyes when I picked her up from the police station. And you sure as fuck wasn't the one wiping away Denver's tears as she sat on the bathroom floor asking why the man she is in love with doesn't feel the same way."

My heart sinks deeper and deeper with every word Spencer speaks. "Tell me what I'm supposed to do, man." I pull at my hair. "I need to get her back. I have to make her forgive me."

Spencer shrugs. "I don't know, Callan. It's not about you. It's about Denver. All I can tell you is that she's heartbroken and doesn't want to see you. Frances and I convinced her to stay over at her place for a while since she doesn't have a home."

"She has a home," I growl.

"Not according to her—or a job, either." Spencer gets a smug look on his face. "However, I remedied that situation. Denver now works for me."

"What the fuck, Spencer. What are you trying to play here?"

"I'm not playing at shit. You have some fucking nerve asking me that. What I'm doing is helping a friend. Not only am I helping Denver, but I'm doing this for you, jackass."

"How is having my woman work for you helping me?"

"Denver doesn't want anything to do with you. Her exact words were, 'I want to move on'. Having Denver working for me keeps her close while your ass figures out how you're going to win her back. If you can." Spencer laughs, and it rubs me the wrong way. The truth fucking stings. Drawing in a calming breath, I listen as he continues. "You have a hell of a lot of groveling to do, Callan."

Sighing, I run my hand through my hair. "Fuck, Spencer. I'll do whatever it takes. I'll fight every day until she's back home where she belongs."

Spencer claps me on the back, and nods. "I have faith you will, man. Denver loves you. She said so herself. You just better pray it's enough." Having eaten the well-deserved ass-chewing Spencer just dished out, and knowing Denver is no longer in jail, I slump into the stool at the counter and run my hand down my face.

"Now, with that out of the way, I came over to let you know Kelly was picked up by the police and charged with making a false claim."

At Spencer's statement, my head snaps up. "What?"

"Yep. It turns out her and Joslyn were cohorts. They devised a plan to get Denver out of the picture."

"Son of a bitch." I stand and start pacing.

"How did you figure out it was them?"

"I didn't. Frances did." Spencer folds his arms across his chest.

"Frances?"

"Yeah, man. You remember last week when Frances left work early for an appointment?" I think for a moment, then nod. "Well, she said she forgot to grab that file you needed. Frances said Kelly was all too eager to drop the file off for her." As Spencer continues to talk all the puzzle pieces begin to fall into place. "She said Kelly asked to use the restroom while she was there. This part is Frances's theory. She believes it gave Kelly ample opportunity to swipe the necklace. So, armed with what information I had, I made a pit stop at Kelly's apartment before coming here." Spencer swaggers across the room. "And me being the badass mother-fucking lawyer I am, Kelly caved in less than five minutes. She confessed everything; threw Joslyn under the bus by saying it was all her idea."

I give Spencer a pointed look. "But it was Kelly who took the necklace from Frances's house and planted the jewelry along with her wallet in Denver's purse."

"Women, man," Spencer shrugs. "It's all she said from this point on."

He's right. No matter how much Joslyn deserves some kind of repercussion, the law won't do anything about it. But, I don't need the law to serve justice. I have connections, and people like to talk.

By the time word gets around, and they find out what she did, Joslyn's modeling career will be over. So will her chances at landing a prospective husband and climbing the social ladder.

Once I realize Spencer is done putting me through the wringer, I try calling Denver's cell. It rings two times before going to voicemail. Fuck.

Not giving up, I call Frances' house, and prepare myself for another ass chewing. I expect Frances to answer, but instead, I get Richard. "Well, son. You screwed the pooch on this one."

I sigh. "Yeah. But I refuse to give up. I'm going to take a guess and say Frances is pissed at me too?"

"You guessed, right. To tell you the truth, so am I."

"I know. I've let a lot of people down. The only thing I can do now is to fix what I have broken. How's she doing, Richard?"

"She's hanging in there. That woman has been through more than she deserves. Denver is a strong woman, Callan. She'll get through this." His words do nothing to lessen the ache in my chest.

"I appreciate you all letting her stay there."

"Not doing it for you. We're doing it for her." Richard clears his throat. "I haven't known her long, but I know enough to realize she's something special."

"She's everything and more," I confess, more to myself than him.

"If that's genuinely how you feel, son, then you have to let the past go. Your father was a shitty man. He not only abandoned your mother, but he left you too. You think you've moved on from what happened when you were a boy, Callan, but you haven't." A heavy sigh comes through the phone. "I've noticed how you hold people at arm's length. Besides me, Frances, and Spencer, you don't allow people to get close enough to let them in. Until Denver came along. Even then, you fought it. I knew the day you brought her to dinner, she was the one for you—the woman who was finally able to break through those steel walls of yours. Your mistake was letting your insecurities and fears overrule your heart. You went into your relationship with Denver with an expiration date hanging over your head." Richard falls quiet for a moment, and I know he's thinking. "She fell head over heels for you, and from my observations, gave all of herself to you, and you held back."

This time when he becomes silent, he does so giving me time to think, and let his words sink in. They do. His truth hits home. *I didn't give Denver everything I had. I held back.*

"I hit the nail on the head, didn't I?" Richard breaks the silence.

I swallow past the huge lump of guilt and remorse stuck in my throat. "Yes," I say, my voice sounding gruff.

"That woman has been through hell and back her entire life. She has not had one person in her whole time on this earth that she could put her trust in and count on other than herself. She has lived her life not having anyone to lean on, to stand up for her, or to love her. Yet she was still able to give all of herself to you and love you. Denver trusted you with something she has never given to another person..." I know what he is about to say. "Her heart." It cuts like a knife, straight into my soul. "What did you do with the gift she gave you?"

My chest tightens as I fight to give my answer. "I broke it."

"You broke it. She didn't use her past as an excuse not to open up and allow herself to love. The betrayal Denver feels is not just the fact that you didn't believe her when she was being accused of something she didn't do; it's the fact you didn't return the same kind of trust and love she has for you."

"I do love her, Richard. I love her more than anything."

"Well, Son. I guess it's time to get off your ass and prove it." Then the line goes dead.

I sit and stew on his words. Everything he said is true. I went into my relationship with Denver believing it would eventually end. Realizing I forgot all about Spencer, I stand. Noticing he's not in the same room as myself, I go in search of him, only to find a yellow sticky note on my front door.

Call me if you need to talk, or help pulling your head out of your ass. Catch you later.

At this moment, there is only one thing I'm sure of; I'm not letting my woman go without a fight. I'm going to earn Denver's trust and win back her heart.

17

DENVER

It wasn't my intention to eavesdrop on Richard's telephone conversation with Callan, but once I knew they were talking about me, I couldn't help myself. Now here I am leaning against the wall outside Richard's office after listening to him lay into Callan.

I guess it's time to get off your ass and prove it.

Just as I'm about to walk away quietly, Richard calls out, "How are you doing, sweetheart?"

I close my eyes and bite my lip. *Shit. I've been made.* Rounding the doorframe, I step into Richard's office. "I'm sorry for listening in on your conversation." I give him a sheepish smile.

Richard waves his hand. "Have a seat." Sitting in a chair across from his desk, I wring my hands in my lap. "What's on your mind, sweetheart?"

I look up from my lap, and take in Richard's concerned face. "You and Callan are close. He once told me you are like a father to him."

Richard's bushy mustache twitches, then his lips turn up in a grin. "I care for Callan very much. Frances and I were not blessed with children of our own, but I consider him and Spencer our sons."

I return a warm smile of my own. "I feel like my being here might come between you all, and despite the way I'm feeling toward Callan now, I would never want my presence to cause any trouble."

"Callan was right. You are something special." Richard leans back in his chair, and clasps his hands together in front of him. "I see why he's in love with you. Despite whatever bullshit life hands you, you still want what's best for others."

"Richard, I..."

He cuts me off. "My wife and I won't accept anything less. Your ass will stay put, sweetheart." I chuckle at Richards playful, no-nonsense vocabulary, and stand.

"Thank you, Richard." I go to leave his office when he calls out.

"Denver."

"Yes?"

"I'm going to speak my piece and then leave whatever happens between you and Callan alone." I give Richard a small nod, letting him know he can continue. "I'm not saying this to take sides. In this particular situation, there can be no sides. But I want you to know Callan acted from a place of fear, and let his past get in the way. Did he tell you about his father?"

"He did," I confirm.

"When I first met Callan as a boy, he was so angry. The older he got, the more the anger turned into determination. That deter-mination is what fueled him to become the successful man he is today— determined to help women stand up to men like his father. But in turn, it also caused him to build a wall around his heart. Callan's fear of abandonment has him keeping people at arm's length. No one has been able to break through those walls until you."

Walking back toward his desk, I sit back down for a moment

while letting Richard's words sink in. "If you're wondering if I'll be able to forgive Callan, then my answer is yes. I will because I love him. The real question is, will I ever be able to look him in the face and not feel the sting of betrayal, and wonder if he would ever do something like this to me again. I want a man who will love me and stand by my side always. A man who I can trust. Right now, I don't trust Callan." Richard says nothing, only nods. His eyes tell me all I need to know. He understands. Giving him a small smile, I leave his office, trying like hell to suppress the gamut of emotions wanting so much to break free. With my own determination, I don't let my love for Callan run over what is more important.

Myself. If I don't protect my own heart, then who will?

Later that evening, after calling Spencer and accepting his job offer, I'm in the kitchen helping Frances with the dinner dishes.

"Frances?"

"Yes?"

"I've already thanked you, but I hope you know how much I appreciate all you have done for me. Not only allowing me to stay in your home until I can find a place of my own but for believing in me. Especially since we haven't known each other very long."

Placing the dish towel on the counter, Frances motions for me to sit with her at the kitchen table. "You don't have to thank me, dear. I knew the day we met you and I would be great friends. My only regret is not knowing your situation when you first started working for Callan. When he told me about the night he found you on the street..." Frances chokes on her words.

Reaching across the table, I lay my hand on hers. "Nothing about that night, or any day before was your fault. It wasn't anyone's fault. If anything, it was mine. It's challenging for me to sit here and take what you, Richard, and Spencer are offering me. It's hard admitting I can't make it on my own; at least for now. I'm finally learning to accept help from people," I assure her.

"Oh, Denver." Frances shakes her head.

"Do you remember the day I had my interview, and you took me to lunch?"

Frances smiles. "I do."

"You'll never know how much you affected my life just by buying me lunch. And later that night at the shelter, I discovered you had put that food in my bookbag." I pause as I try to control my emotions.

"It had been two days since I had eaten, and it was like you knew."

At my confession, Frances starts to cry. "I just figured you were going through a rough patch financially. I could sense you were hungry but declined my offer for lunch. I sensed something that day but had no idea how dire your situation was. Had I known..."

I stop her. "I know; you probably would have taken me home with you that day." I smile.

"Your damn right, I would." Frances and I are quiet for a minute as we gather ourselves. Just then, Spencer strides into the kitchen, and takes in mine and Frances's state.

"Is this a bad time?"

"No, no. Come on in," Frances answers.

"Good, because I have some news." He smiles. "The charges against you have been dropped," Spencer addresses me.

"Oh my god!" I jump out of the chair. "How?"

"Kelly."

I look to Frances then back to Spencer. "So, Frances was right?"

"Indeed, she was," Spencer confirms.

Richard strolls into the kitchen. "That's because my woman is quite the investigator. She can spot a bullshitter a mile away."

"Oh, hush." Frances swats at her husband.

I turn my attention back to Spencer. "So, what happens now?"

"Well, while Kelly has the pleasure of spending the night in the same jail cell you did, you get to move forward and hopefully put the whole incident behind you."

"What about Joslyn? What is her punishment?"

Spencer sighs. "Unfortunately, nothing. Even though Kelly admits she and Joslyn were in on it together, it was Kelly who planted the wallet and jewelry then called the police with the false allegations."

"That's not fair." I purse my lips. "Joslyn conspired with Kelly to set me up. That has to count for something."

"We all agree, sweetheart. But in this case, it's Kelly's word against Joslyn," Richard clarifies the legalities of it all.

"Don't worry, Denver." Spencer places his hand on my shoulder. "Callan won't let her get away with it for too long."

"So, he knows it was Kelly and Joslyn?" More hurt begins to settle in my stomach as the entire story unfolds. How do people become so petty and vindictive?

"Yes. I stopped by his apartment earlier."

"At least he believes me now," I mutter under my breath. Nobody says anything about my off-handed comment. I'm not quite ready to move past my bitchy stage and into forgiveness when it comes to Callan. Stepping up to Spencer, I hug him and kiss his cheek. "Thanks for handling the whole debacle for me. I don't know how I'll repay you."

Spencer squeezes me. "You agreed to be my assistant. That's good enough for me. My office and calendar are complete and utter chaos."

"I guess I'll see you first thing in the morning then?" I smile.

"Denver, you don't have to start tomorrow. Why don't you take the rest of the week off? Come in on Monday."

"No." I shake my head. "I'd much rather keep myself busy. So, if tomorrow is okay with you, I'll see you in the morning." Spencer agrees. "I'll see you tomorrow then."

Later that night, I am lying in bed when my phone begins to ring. Callan's name pops up on the screen, and I immediately send it to voicemail again, even though I want nothing more than to hear his voice. A second later, the phone vibrates with a text message.

Callan: I'm sorry, baby. I fucked up.

Callan: Please answer your phone.

Callan: I need to hear your voice.

Callan: I miss you.

A tear slides down my cheek onto the phone screen as I read Callan's words. I can't bring myself to reply. No matter how bad I want to. "I miss you too." Setting my phone on the table beside the bed, I hug a pillow into my chest and curl into a ball. I don't know how long I lay crying before sleep finally sneaks in and rescues me from the heartache I'm struggling to break free from.

THE NEXT MORNING, I wake to find some, but not all of my clothes from Callan's Penthouse delivered. I'm guessing Spencer told him about my new job. Deciding not to question Callan's gesture, I go about getting ready for my first day of work. After securing my long hair back in a fishtail braid, I put on a pair of black high waisted, wide-leg dress slacks, a cream color blouse, and pair it with some brown ankle boots with a three-inch heel. Stepping in front of the mirror, I take in my reflection. As I look at myself wearing the clothes Callan bought me, a small part of me wants to be petty and toss all the clothes in the trash. Like I did my purse. What can I say? I was having a moment. Spending the night in jail does something to a woman.

"I really shouldn't have tossed the purse," I sigh.

Noticing the time, I realize the Uber taking me to work will be here any minute, and I grab my things and head downstairs, where I find Frances about to head out herself. "Good morning, Denver. I was just about to get you. I'm going to drop you at work."

"That's kind of you, Frances, but Spencer's office is in the opposite direction. I already called an Uber." Then I get an alert; my ride's here. "See. My ride just pulled up."

"Okay, dear. If you're sure."

"Yep. I'll see you later." I wave as I walk toward the door. I'm just about to head out when Frances stops me.

"Wait! Before I forget." She pulls something from her pocket, handing it to me. "Here's a key to the house and the code for the alarm."

"Thanks." I pocket the key.

As I make it down the steps toward my waiting ride, I notice a black sedan parked on the street and a man talking to the Uber driver. A second later, my ride drives off and the other man steps up to the sedan, opening the back door. "Miss Hollis, Mr. Hawk sent me to accompany you to and from work."

I narrow my eyes at Mitch. "Did he now?"

"Yes, ma'am. Along with anywhere else you wish to go."

Letting out a frustrated breath, I peer down at my watch. Crap. Not wanting to be late for work, I relent. "Fine," I climb into the back seat. As Mitch shuts the door, I look to my left and find a cup of Starbucks coffee sitting in the cupholder; next to it, a small white bag. Reaching over, I snatch the bag and peek inside to find a cinnamon bun still warm. I pick up the coffee to take a sip, stopping short when I read *I miss you* written on the side of the cup in Callan's handwriting. Between the clothes, and car, it only takes those three little words to make my heart flutter.

Fifteen minutes later, the car pulls up in front of Spencer's building, which is just as big as the one Callan owns. "Would you like me to walk you in, ma'am?" Mitch asks when he opens the door, letting me out.

"No, thank you, Mitch. And please call me Denver."

Mitch chuckles. "Will do. Have a good day, Denver. I'll be back at four-thirty to take you home."

Unlike Callan, when I walk into Spencer's building, instead of security, I'm met by a woman who looks to be in her seventies sitting behind a computer at a large desk.

"Hello, young lady. Can I help you?"

"Yes, ma'am. Would you tell me what floor Spencer Knight is on?"

"He's at the top. Twentieth floor."

"Thank you."

"You're welcome, young lady."

After riding the elevator to the top, the doors open, revealing complete chaos. "Goddammit, Jonathan, where is Judy? And where the hell is my eight o'clock?" Spencer's voice reverberates off the walls. I've never heard Spencer use that tone, let alone raise his voice. A skinny guy wearing a brown sweater vest and glasses stammers as he answers my new boss' question.

"It...it's just now eight, Sir."

I walk past several people bustling about the office as I make my way across the room. Including the man I now know as Jonathan, who whispers, "run," as he rushes past me.

"Jonathan!" Spencer yells again as he rounds the corner, almost running me over.

I grin. "Hi, boss."

"Hey, sweetheart. You didn't happen to see a skinny dude wearing glasses, did you?"

"No?" I lift a brow, trying to give my new coworker a head start.

"Saving your coworkers from the asshole boss already. They'll love you around here." Spencer grins.

"Looks like I showed up just in time too. If you show me to my desk, I'll get started. Lucky for you, Frances trained me, so I know how to hold my own."

Three hours later, I finally finish going through and organizing Spencer's calendar and rescheduled at least a dozen appointments that were double booked. Then filtered through and responded to all his unopened emails, had his dry cleaning delivered, and ran interference between him and Jonathan twice. I just finished setting up the conference room for his two-thirty meeting and ordered him lunch, which should arrive in thirty minutes. Plopping down in my chair, I enjoy the silence. Spencer wasn't wrong when he said I would be doing him a favor and saving his ass.

Spencer steps out of his office with a look of awe on his face. "I don't know what miracle you performed, but let it be known, I'm never letting you leave."

I laugh. "I'm glad I could be of service. Although I wasn't sure I could pull it off. Frances has Callan's office run like a well-oiled machine. There wasn't a whole lot for me to do there. Now this," I say, pointing around the office, "was a disaster."

"Excuse me." Spencer and I are interrupted by a delivery guy holding a huge vase full of two dozen red roses. "I have a delivery for Denver Hollis."

"That's me," I as I raise my hand and stand from my desk. The man hands the flowers to me, and I set them on my desk. "Have a good day."

"You too," I say as I gaze at the roses taking up half my workstation.

"Looks like the son of a bitch is already trying to take you from me." Spencer smirks.

I roll my eyes and try to feign being annoyed but fail as I quickly pluck the card from the arrangement. *I'm never not thinking of you.* I'd be lying if I said all of Callan's small gestures today haven't made my tummy flutter. Not two seconds after reading the card, another delivery guy, the same young man who always delivers Callan's lunch, Dillon shows up holding a white back with TARANTINO'S scrolled across it.

"Let me guess. You're looking for Denver Hollis," Spencer huffs in annoyance.

"Hi, Dillon," I greet him.

"Miss Hollis, your lunch."

I take the bag from him. "Thank you," I reply, holding the bag as I watch a grinning Dillion eye Spencer before crossing the room on his way to the elevator. Spencer chuckles beside me, and I cut my eyes at him, waiting for him to say something. Anything.

"I'll leave you to eat your lunch, sweetheart." Spencer retreats into his office, leaving me more confused than ever. How am I supposed to move on when the one person I'm running from is chasing me? Maybe I want to be caught. Either way, Callan Hawk is making it hard not to love him.

18

DENVER

"Are you sure you don't want to come with Richard and me to my sister's? She'd be happy to have you," Frances asks as she and Richard load their bags into the trunk of their car. They're headed to spend Christmas with her sister in New Jersey and will be gone for three days. "I don't like the idea of you being alone for a holiday."

I'm quick to reassure her. "I'll be fine. Besides, I plan on spending Christmas day helping down at the shelter. They could always use the extra volunteers this time of year. You two go ahead and have a good time. Don't worry about me."

Frances' face softens as she pulls me in for a hug. Out of the corner of my eye, I notice Richard stepping away to make a phone call. "If you need anything, don't hesitate to call. Spencer is going to be in town so, call him too if you need anything. He can be here in no time," France reminds me for the third time this morning.

My heart warms at the thought of someone caring whether or not I'm alone. That's not something I've had before. Ending his call, Richard steps up to me and kisses my cheek, his mustache tickling my skin. "See ya, sweetheart."

"Bye, Richard. Drive safe and let me know you made it." I wave as the two of them climb into the car. When they are no longer in sight, I head back inside the house, where I jog up the stairs to my room. Kicking off my slippers, I strip out of my plaid pajamas and into a pair of jeans, black sweater, and tennis shoes. With all that has been going on, I missed Roland's birthday party. So, today, I am going by the library in hopes he is working. Stuffing my phone and keys into the pocket of my coat, I pull my hat on over my head and leave. With it being Christmas Eve, I don't bother with calling Mitch, opting for a taxi instead.

Walking into the library, a huge smile takes over my face when I see Roland. He recognizes me immediately and returns a smile of his own. "Denver. It's so good to see you."

"You too. I hope it's okay that I'm dropping by like this. It's just that I missed your party and wanted to tell you in person, happy belated birthday."

"Of course, it's alright. Come, sit down." He ushers me to an empty table. "How have you been? Lucas tells me you got that job at his office. He also says his boss fancies you." He waggles his bushy eyebrows.

I force a smile on my face at the mention of Callan. "I got the job. All thanks to you. That's another reason I came here. I wanted to thank you for helping me."

Roland pats my arm. "No need to thank me, young lady. You got that job all on your own." He spreads his arms, gesturing at me. "Now, look at you."

"Granddad?" A voice calls from behind. Twisting in my chair, I watch as Lucas strides in our direction. His eyes land on me sitting with Roland, and grins. "Denver, what are you doing here?"

"I stopped by for a visit, but I was just leaving."

"Are you in a hurry to get somewhere? I dropped by to give granddad a ride home. But if you don't have a place to be, we can grab dinner or something," he says hopefully.

"Oh, you two go on. Your mother is picking me up today. She's taking me to do some last-minute shopping."

Lucas' dimples make an appearance when he beams at me. "What do you say, Denver?"

I bite my lip, not sure if I should accept his offer. "Sure. Dinner sounds good."

The moment we exit the library, I'm shocked to see Mitch parked at the curb waiting expectantly. "Miss Hollis." His eyes cut to Lucas.

"What are you doing here, Mitch?" I roll my eyes. This is not cool. It feels like I'm being spied on, and I don't like it.

"I was sent to pick you up, Miss H—I mean Denver," he corrects himself when I give him a stern look.

"I didn't call you." I fold my arms, letting him know I'm not happy.

"Mr. Hawk said I would find you here."

"He did, did he? How did Callan know where I was?" I ask bewildered then stop short when the answer pops into my head. "He's tracking my phone, isn't he?" Mitch's silence is all the answer I need. I turn to Lucas. "Did you drive here?"

Lucas points down the street. "I'm parked down the block."

I turn back to Mitch. "I'm sorry you wasted your time coming all this way, Mitch, but I won't be needing a ride. Be sure to tell Mr. Hawk as well."

Mitch's lip twitches. "Not a problem, Denver."

After Lucas and I climb into his car, he cocks his head to the side. "You know this probably won't bode well for me?"

My expression turns serious. "We don't have to go to dinner, Lucas. I can get a cab home. I don't want to cause you any trouble."

"And miss my chance at hanging out with a beautiful woman? Not a chance."

Fifteen minutes later, Lucas and I sit at a table in a quaint little Greek restaurant. The waitress places our menus in front of us.

"Can I start you off with something to drink?"

"I'll have water."

"I'll have whatever beer you have on tap," Lucas tells the waitress.

I glance over the menu. "What do you suggest? I don't think I've ever eaten Greek food before."

"Do you trust me to order for you?" he asks, and I nod. When the waitress returns, Lucas orders for the two of us.

"Great. I'll have your order out soon."

Once the waitress walks off, Lucas gets right to what I was expecting him to bring up. "Denver, I wanted to say I'm sorry for how things played out with Kelly."

"Why are you sorry? You didn't do anything." His apology leaves me puzzled.

"Yeah, but I stood by along with everyone else and said nothing while that bitch accused you of stealing. So that you know, no one at the office believed what Kelly was accusing you of. Even before the truth came out."

"Though unnecessary, I appreciate you saying that, Lucas."

"And just so you know, the office is not the same without you either. Mr. Hawk isn't the same either," he adds.

A few minutes later, our food is delivered and just as I am about to dive in, my phone starts ringing. Pulling it from my pocket, I notice Callan's name lighting up the screen, and send the call to voicemail.

"Sorry," I say to Lucas, who gives me a knowing look.

Two seconds later, my phone starts ringing again. This time I cut it off and shove it back into my coat pocket. No sooner do I put my phone away than Lucas' phone starts ringing. I close my eyes. *Please don't let that be Callan.*

Lucas looks down at his cell then back at me. He answers. "Hello?" I watch as Lucas listens to Callan's voice on the other end. "I'm kind of in the middle of a date, boss. Can it wait?" Callan's booming voice carries through Lucas' cell, loud enough for the people seated near us to turn their heads in our direction. I begin to worry about Lucas getting into trouble. By the way, his shoulders start shaking as he holds back his laughter, it becomes apparent he is not the least bit concerned with his boss' tirade. "Sure thing, Mr. Hawk. I'll see you soon." He hangs up. "Looks like my boss left the Kerrigan file at the office, and I'm the only one who can bring it to him," Lucas smirks, not at all hiding his amusement.

My shoulders slump, and I rest my forehead in my hand. "I'm sorry, Lucas. He's being a jerk because of me."

"No. He's acting like a man who does whatever it takes to keep his woman away from another man," Lucas says with a bit of admiration in his voice.

"You and I are friends." I throw my hands up. "Can't he see that?"

Lucas chuckles. "Yeah. But if you ever give me an opening, Denver, I wouldn't hesitate to take it, and Callan knows that."

"What?" I squeak.

"Don't be dense, sweetheart. Sure, we're friends, but you're a sexy as fuck woman, and I'd be an idiot not to take whatever you'd be willing to offer. I'm also a man who knows when he doesn't stand a chance. I did have fun fucking with Callan, though. Even if he's going to make my life hell at the office."

"I'm...I..." *Am I really being dense?*

Lucas stands and tosses a few bills on the table. "Come on, sweetheart. I'll walk you out." He places his hand on the small of my back, ushering me out of the restaurant where Mitch is waiting. Again, I roll my eyes. He steps out of the driver's seat with his cell to his ear—no doubt talking to Callan. Mitch remains on the phone as he steps around to the back passenger side and opens the door for me. Lucas gets a little gleam in his eye as he leans in and places a kiss on my cheek. "We'll have to try this again some other time, sweetheart," Lucas says the words a lot louder than necessary, and I know it's meant for Callan to hear. Why must he egg him on?

I step to the car. "Mitch," I say in a flat, uninterested tone. This time, Mitch clears his throat, fighting through a chuckle. He quickly composes himself as I sink into the back seat, and he closes the door.

THE NEXT AFTERNOON, I'm at the shelter helping serve food when Lucy comes in with her hands full, so I rush to help her.

"Here, let me help."

"Denver! Oh my god! It's been forever since I've seen you."

Lucy and I set the bags down on the table we have set up to serve the food, and pull each other in for a hug.

"I've been worried about you. The last time I saw you was when that man skipped town with your money. Are you still working for that lawyer?"

"Uh, actually, I'm working for his friend now. As his assistant." I keep my answer light.

"That's cool. What about an apartment? Did you ever find one? You must have since I haven't seen you around here."

"I found a place." I decide to be vague, not giving her too much information. Changing the subject, I ask. "What about you? How's school? Are you enjoying the holidays?" I finish laying the bread out on the table.

"I am. I'm leaving with some friends of mine tomorrow. We're going to spend New Year's in Florida. But, before catching my flight later this morning, I wanted to drop off all this extra food we had at my parents' house. No need for it to go to waste."

"That was thoughtful of you, Lucy." My compliment earns me a smile. Over the next hour, Lucy and I work side by side along with the other volunteers, serving dozens of men, women and children who are standing in line waiting for a hot meal. The number of people in need today was more than the shelter has experienced so far this year, and what's worse, is we are running out of food, fast. I look at Lucy. "They're still so many people to feed. What are we going to do?" A commotion at the entrance of the shelter grabs both our attention. Lifting on my toes, I try peering over the people still standing in line to catch a glimpse of what's going on. The shelter's coordinator, Carol, bustles toward us with several men trailing behind her, all carrying trays of precooked food. One after another, the men set the food down on the table in front of us and the waiting people. There is so much food we are forced to set up three extra tables. "Where did all this come from?" I ask in awe.

Carol points across the room. "The handsome young man, standing over there." She points across the room and my eyes follow her line of sight, and cover my mouth, holding a gasp back, the moment I spot Callan. He's helping some of the men set up tables. As if he feels my gaze, Callan stops what he's doing and turns. His eyes land directly on mine.

At this moment, I let my heart lead me. Without hesitation, my feet carry me toward him, my heart pounding like a drum. Callan drops the chair he was carrying, meeting me halfway. I don't say anything as I throw myself into his arms. This is what matters; not the flowers, lunches, or the car. Not even the little notes that made my stomach flutter. This right here, his grand act of human kindness does me in.

He wraps his arms tight around me, and I cling to him as if he's the only lifeline I have in this world. "Fuck, baby. I've missed holding you," he rasps as I bury my face in his neck. I breathe him in, clutching at his neck collar as if I'm terrified he'll disappear. We hold each other for a long moment before I step back, breaking the connection. I can tell he's reluctant to let me go but does so anyway. I am grateful for his actions here today, but I don't want him thinking this will erase what he's done. A tiny shred of guilt seeps into the pit of my stomach when I see a flicker of hurt dance across Callan's face when my head starts overthinking things again, and I take a step back, putting distance between us.

"This is amazing, Callan. How were you able to get all this food last minute?"

The cocky grin I love so much makes an appearance. "I have my ways."

"Money talks." I don't mean for my words to come out sounding callous. A wounded look crosses Callan's face, and my stomach falls. Seeing him hurt, because of my words makes me feel horrible inside.

"Money does tend to help." I hear the slight upset in his voice.

"I'm sorry, Callan. I didn't mean it like that." I reach out to touch him but stop myself.

"I know you didn't." The lines on Callan's face soften, as do his eyes. We both fall silent for a minute, neither quite sure what to say. "Listen, Denver. I..."

I hold up my hand. "Not here. I don't want to talk about it here. Today has been a good day, and with your generous help, it has gotten a whole lot better. Let's focus on that and helping as many people as we can instead."

Callan gives me a tight-lipped nod. "Will you allow me to drive you home later?" My eyes fall to the floor. "Please, baby," Callan pleads.

The moment the endearment passes his lips, my tummy gets that all too familiar flutter. I think about his request for a moment and decide we both have things we need to get off our chests. "Okay."

Callan visibly relaxes. "Yeah?" He looks for clarifications, and I nod, giving him a small smile. He sighs. "Thank you. I'll be here all day helping. Come find me when you're done."

The rest of the day passes in a quick blur. My head is a

jumbled mess, and my nerves have kicked in when I realize it's almost time to leave for the day. "You ready to go, baby?" Callan asks, stepping up to me as he pulls his coat on.

I lick my lips. "Yeah. Let me say goodbye to Carol really quick." Callan has my jacket in his hands, and helps me slip in on.

"I'll wait here," he whispers in my ear, the heat of his breath prickles my skin, and I have to fight the urge to spin around and kiss him like a fool.

Making my way into the back, I find Carol in the kitchen. "Hey. I'm heading out. Do you need anything before I go?"

Carol stops what she's doing. "We got it from here, Denver. Go on home with that hunk of man meat I saw you with earlier. Tell him thank you for me again."

I blush. "I'll tell him," then turn to leave, but Carol stops me.

"Hey, Denver. I think what you did today was great. I'm happy you've been able to get back on your feet."

"You're welcome, Carol. I'll forever be grateful for what you all do here, and what you've done for me. I promise to come back and help as often as I can." We both smile at one another before she resumes what she was doing, and I exit the room.

When I emerge from the back, Callan is still rooted where he said he'd wait for me. Stopping beside him, he reaches out, placing his palm on the small of my back, leading me outside to his car. Callan opens the door and I climb in. His scent is all around me as I settle in the seat. Closing my eyes, I take in a deep breath, letting the smell of him fill my senses.

Callan sits beside me, leaving a small space between us, as the car moves down the road. Our hands rest on the leather seat, and my fingers twitch because I want so badly to touch him. The tension in the car becomes palpable on the drive home. The air thickens with so many emotions I can feel the weight of it pressing against my body. It's not until Callan parks in front of Frances and Richard's townhouse does he speak. "I'm sorry, Denver," Callan says those words to me, his green eyes boring into my soul. I know he means it. "I know I've texted you those words a dozen times in the past week. I also know words will never be enough. I can promise you, baby; I'm going to do everything in my power to earn your trust back." He palms my cheek and I lean into his touch. "I love you, Denver Hollis." With those three words spoken, the flood gates open. It's like I've taken my first breath of air.

"I love you too, Callan. I love you so much, but...I need time." My last words hurt, but they are my truth.

"I'm going to give you all the time you need. "

Tears fall down my cheeks. "I still haven't forgiven you." I sniffle. "I trusted you, Callan. I followed your lead when it came to our relationship, even though I knew we were moving too fast. I voiced my concerns several times, but in the end, I trusted you enough to fall. I fell so deeply in love with you, Callan, and I thought you felt the same." Callan pulls a handkerchief from his pocket, and dries my tears. I keep talking, needing him to hear me. I need him to understand. "When I needed you the most, you weren't there. I thought I had gone into this whirlwind relationship with eyes wide open. I feel so stupid for actually being so blind to the fact that you really didn't give us your all." I take a shuttered breath.

"I love you so fucking much, Denver. I know now that I've allowed my past and insecurities to cloud my judgment and my heart. I can promise you that it will never happen again."

I hiccup, trying to gain better control of my emotions. "I want to believe you. I do." My red-rimmed eyes stay fixed on Callan. "I was so scared, Callan. I'd never been arrested before. Having an officer put handcuffs on me, being placed into the back of a squad car, in broad daylight with strangers gawking at me. Being questioned and then having to sleep in a cold cell." Pausing for a moment to catch my breath, I look out the car window. "You want to know the worst part? Having the man I love, who I thought cared about me, look at me like I was nothing. Having that memory embedded in my soul is what keeps me from not being able to move forward. No matter how bad I want to move on with you, I'm scared."

"All I'm asking for today is a chance. Let me prove it to you, Denver. You can trust me again," he emphasizes. "We can take things as slow or as fast as you want. You're in the driver's seat, baby. I need you like I need air to breathe. I'll put in the work, and do whatever it takes," Callan chokes out. The pain and sincerity in his voice settle deep in my core.

"How?" I ask. "How do we make this work?"

"We start over. I didn't do it right the first time, and I intend to make it right." Callan clears his voice. "Denver, would you go out with me?"

"You want to take me on a date?"

"Yes."

I mull over his question, making him wait several agonizing minutes until I give him my answer. "Okay." "Saturday, at seven?" he asks hopefully.

I nod. "Okay."

19

DENVER

It's a Saturday night, and I'm getting ready for my date with Callan. It has been three days since our talk in his car, and every day since he has called me. Callan and I both acknowledged this was the part of our relationship we had skipped over. We are getting to know each other. We spend hours on the phone. A smile tugs at my lips as I slip on my heels. We've talked about everything. I've opened up to him a little more about my past and my time in foster care, and listened to him tell me countless stories about his mom. Getting to know the man behind the suit, is giving us a solid foundation to move forward with our relationship. My head still has a little catching up to do, and Callan realizes it will take time, but my heart, without a doubt, never stopped loving him.

The sound of the doorbell brings me out of my thoughts. Stepping in front of the floor-length mirror, I take in my reflection and hope Callan likes it as much as I do. I found the dress for a steal at a vintage thrift shop Frances introduced me to. After work yesterday she insisted on taking me shopping for a new dress for my date. Frances was so excited, I agreed. I'm glad I did. Frances and I have formed a bond. She, in a way, is like the mother I never had. It feels good having that kind of motherly love. It makes me feel special. Frances cried when I told her as much.

Twirling, I admire the way the dress fits my body. It's a simple black lace, off the shoulder, knee length, cocktail dress. The red peep-toe heels, I paired with it, give the outfit the perfect pop of color. There's a knock on the bedroom door, followed by Frances peeking her head in.

"Hey, Denver. Callan is downstairs," Frances says just before she takes in my dress, and her eyes light up. "Oh! I knew this was going to look stunning on you."

"Thanks." I smooth my palms down the front.

"Oh!" Frances claps her hands. "Wait here, dear. I have just the thing to go with this beautiful dress. I'll be right back."

Frances dashes out of the room and returns a minute later, holding a square black velvet box in her hand. Standing in front of me, she opens it revealing a pair of ruby earrings. I gasp, placing my hand over my mouth. "Frances, no. I couldn't possibly wear these." The sparkle from the small diamonds surrounding the ruby hypnotizes me. Frances takes the earrings from the box and proceeds to put them on me.

"Of course you can. These earrings belonged to my mother. And my grandmother before her. My mother gave them to me when I was twenty years old as I was getting ready for my first date with Richard. She told me to give them to my daughter when she went on her first date with the man she was going to spend the rest of her life with." Frances' voice trembles as she talks. "I think of you as a daughter, Denver." She turns me, so I'm facing the mirror. My eyes meet her kind ones in our reflection. She squeezes my shoulder. "I would be honored if you allow me to pass such a gift down to you, so long as you continue the same tradition with your first daughter." Butterflies swarm in my tummy, and my heart swells at the thought of having children with Callan.

Turning, I hug Frances. "I'd be honored to wear them and carry on the tradition." I wipe the tears falling down my face.

"Come on, dear. No more tears, or you're going to ruin your makeup." Frances ushers me along. "Come on. We don't want you to be late for your dinner reservation." I follow Frances out of the bedroom. As I make my way down the stairs, my eyes go straight to Callan's. The moment my foot touches the last step, he smiles. "I'm a lucky son of a bitch."

Richard strolls into the living room where Callan is standing. "What's this I hear about you wanting to take my Denver on a date?"

Callan's lip twitches as he respectfully plays along. "Yes, Sir. I'm taking my girl out on the town."

"And what time do you plan on having her home?"

"I don't know, Richard. I hadn't planned that far ahead." Callan never takes his eyes off me.

"I'll plan for you then, Son. I want Denver back home by ten o'clock." Callan tries to suppress a smirk, while I try to hide my giggle.

"Richard. What in the Sam hell are you doing?" Frances chastises her husband. "Let them be."

"Woman, don't ruin my fun. I never got to play this part before," Richard playfully warns his wife, and tugs her into his side. Frances loses her scowl, and my heart warms at how much he wants to look out for me.

Callan crosses the room, taking me by the hand. His touch is feeding the spark and igniting a flame. My entire body comes to life, and I interlock my fingers with his.

"Hold up!" Richard pipes up. "Let me go upstairs and get my shotgun. Then I can start over and do this right." Richard turns on his heel.

"He's not serious, is he?" I laugh as I watch Richard retreat up the stairs.

Frances gives me a look. "Oh, he's dead serious. The old coot has lost his mind. You two kids get on out of here before he comes back. There's no telling what other shenanigans that man has up his sleeves." She does her best to look serious, but laughter overtakes her in her final words. "You'd better hurry."

Mitch is waiting for us next to Callan's car the moment we step out into the cold night air. "Good evening, Denver."

"Hi, Mitch." I smile as he opens the car door. Callan stops me before I climb in. Slipping his arm around my waist, he pulls my body flush against his. "You steal my breath away." His lips hover above mine.

"Thank you."

"I know it's customary to wait until the end of the date to ask for a kiss." Callan's eyes fall to my red-painted lips. "But, I'd very much like to kiss you now." His minty breath mixes with mine, waiting for me to say yes.

I lick my lips. "Okay," is the only word I can produce at the moment, and Callan's lips press softly against mine. The kiss is understated, yet passionate. The way a kiss on the first date should be.

It's been a few weeks since Callan and I officially got back together. Much to his dismay, I'm still living with Frances and Richard. I'm also still working for Spencer. He asks me every day to come home, but I decline. Honestly, I don't know what's holding me back. A small part of me fears the unknown and putting my trust in him again.

So far, Callan has been the model boyfriend. Mitch still picks me up every morning. Lunch is still promptly delivered to my desk at noon, and Callan is always waiting outside Spencer's building to take me home at the end of each workday. He sees to my every need, proving he is determined to take care of me.

I sense Callan is at his tipping point. I feel that at any moment, he is going to scoop me up caveman-style and carry me back to his penthouse. And as I sit here in the stall of the women's bathroom at work, staring down at the positive pregnancy test, in my hand, I know without a doubt Callan will take care of his baby too. Butterflies swarm in my stomach at the thought of being a mother, and I smile. I have the best people in my life and can say with certainty this baby will be so loved. I'm going to give my son or daughter everything I never had.

Later that night, Callan and Spencer are here at Frances and Richard's to celebrate Richard's retirement. There is a big party planned next weekend, but tonight Richard wanted to celebrate with us, his family. Callan, who is sitting beside me, stands and lifts his glass of Champagne. "It's about time you start living life doing whatever the hell you want. I can't think of any man who deserves it more. You've dedicated your entire career to helping others. You find the good in people and do your best to help them see it too. I know Spencer would agree when I say, if it weren't for you, we wouldn't be where we are today." Callan glances down at me, with love in his eyes. "You helped me pull my head out my ass more times than I'd like to admit and showed me the paths worth taking. You're my mentor, the man I look up to. You've shown me what a man can and should be. I love you, Richard, and hope one day to be half the man you are." We all lift our glasses in the air. "Show off." Spencer eyes Callan with a smirk, and I giggle.

As Callan takes his seat, he notices I have yet to touch my drink, and asks, "Your champagne warm, baby? Want me to get you another glass?"

"No, no." I pause, trying to produce an excuse for not drinking. With tonight's focus on Richard's accomplishments, I don't want to bring up my news.

"I think she's coming down with something," Spencer cuts in. "She's been looking a little green all week. I've even seen her making extra trips to the restroom at work."

Shit!

Callan scoots his chair back, suddenly full of worry. "Baby. You didn't mention you weren't feeling well. I'll give Dr. Morgan a call." Callan pulls his cell phone from his pocket and begins dialing.

I put my hand over his, stopping him from making the call. "Callan. Put the phone away. I'm not sick."

"Are you sure? You do look a little pale, baby."

"Callan, I'm not sick. I'm pregnant." The words slip from my mouth. Frances gasps and Spencer mutters, "Holy shit."

Callan, however, goes stock still, his expression I can't decipher. My nerves kick in. Unmoving, I wait for his reaction with bated breath.

Suddenly dropping to his knees, Callan wraps his arms around my torso and lays his forehead against my belly. Quiet tears trickle down Frances' cheeks, and Richard pulls her close. I thread my fingers through Callan's soft, dark hair. My nervousness vanishes entirely as the man I love continues to hold me. "Not exactly the way I wanted to tell you we're having a baby," I say. Callan lifts his head, and I take in his devastatingly handsome face. I smile at him, losing myself like I always do in his tantalizingly green eyes. I hope our baby has his eyes.

"A beautiful woman walked into my office once. She stole my heart before I ever knew her name." Tears fall from my eyes, landing on Callan's cheek as he holds my gaze. "Now, she's giving me the greatest gift I could ever imagine." He palms my stomach. "I love you, baby."

"I love you too." My hand covers his, and I tell him, "I'm ready to come home."

Callan stands and pulls me into him. "For good?"

"For good," I confirm, and for a moment, the room falls silent.

"Well, what the hell are you waiting for?" Richard throws his hands in the air. "Kiss her already."

Callan kisses my forehead, then takes my face in the palms of his hands. He hovers his lips inches from mine. "I plan on keeping you forever, Denver Hollis. Marry me?"

I close my eyes. "Okay." Then my man kisses me.

EPILOGUE

ONE YEAR LATER

I wake to hear the soft sounds of baby whimpers coming through the monitor sitting on the bedside table. Not wanting to wake Callan, I carefully lift his arm from around my waist. Slipping from his hold, I climb out of the bed. I quietly pad down the hall to the nursery, push open the door, and make my way over to the crib.

"Hey, little man," I coo at Jacob, whose big bright green eyes gaze back at me.

Reaching down, I scoop him up and cradle him close to my chest. Placing my nose to his cheek, I inhale his sweet baby scent as I walk over to the rocking chair that sits in front of the window. Once settled into the chair, I lower my gown's left side, allowing Jacob to latch onto my breast eagerly. Rocking back and forth, I gently stroke the smattering of red hair on the top of his head and watch as his eyes stare up at me. Quiet moments like this are my favorite.

A few months ago, Callan and I welcomed our son into the world. Jacob Callan Hawk weighed in at seven pounds and ten ounces. Jacob inherited his father's eyes and features, but his red hair is all me. When I discovered I was pregnant, I feared becoming a mother and being responsible for another human being. Irrational thoughts kept plaguing me. *What if I became homeless again? How would I care for my son living on the streets? How would I feed and clothe him?* It didn't take me long to work through my insecurities. I'm committed to Callan. I had to trust he would take care of our son and me, and never let anything happen to us.

When I moved back in with Callan, he was terrific at showing me how much he loved me and was doing everything in his power to right the wrongs he had made at the beginning of our relationship. I soon realized I owed him the same by trusting in him and us. Once I did that, I finally let go, and my fears eventually melted away. I gave myself entirely to the man I love, and in return, he gave himself to me.

"Hey," Callan whispers, stepping into the room.

"Hi." I tear my eyes away from Jacob, who is now fast asleep, and smile up at my husband, leaning against the doorframe, shirtless, and wearing a pair of grey sweatpants that are sitting low on his hips. The man still makes my tummy flutter.

I drink in the sight of him as he strolls across the room. Stopping in front of me, Callan gently takes our son from my arms, walks over to his crib, and kisses his forehead before laying him down. Striding back to me, he takes my hand and pulls me from the rocking chair and leads me back down the hall to our bedroom.

After getting back together, Callan didn't waste any time making me his wife. Ten months ago, we got married in an intimate ceremony in Frances and Richard's backyard. Spencer was

Callan's best man, Frances was my Matron of Honor, and Richard gave me away.

The day was perfect.

Besides the birth of our son, it was the happiest day of my life. Soon after we were married, Callan put the apartment on the market and bought us a three-bedroom townhouse with a yard. The best thing about it is our house is on the same street where Richard and Frances live.

Stopping next to the bed, Callan lifts the cover and waits for me to lie down. Once I do, he climbs in behind me, pulling me flush against him, my back to his chest.

"Did you remember to set the alarm?" I ask.

Callan releases a heavy sigh. "Why don't you call Spencer in the morning and tell him to find his own damn secretary? It's not like he can't find someone else," Callan grumbles.

"I promised him I would vet those who applied for the position and set up the interviews. The temp agency has run out of people to send since he's fired the last five women they sent him."

I ended up working for Spencer up until two weeks before my due date. After Jacob was born, I decided I wanted to be a stay-at-home mom for a while. Callan was one hundred percent on-board with the idea, but Spencer was less than enthusiastic about losing me. I even set up a replacement for him before I quit, but she only lasted a week. In the past three and a half months, Spencer has gone through six secretaries. Last week I offered to go over the two dozen or so applications he's received for the position and help him with the interviews.

"It should only take me a week or so to hire someone. Besides, Frances is over the moon with getting to watch Jacob for me this week."

"Did you forget Frances helps keep me organized at the office? I had to give her the week off so you can help Spencer. How the hell does that make sense? That asshole has inconvenienced us all because his grumpy ass can't keep a secretary for more than a week."

I giggle. "You leave Spencer up to me. I will find someone who is not afraid to stand up to him and won't put up with his crap. What Spencer needs is someone who's not afraid to bite back."

"Fine," Callan huffs. "One week. That's all he gets."

The two of us fall silent for a moment before I speak again. "Thank you."

Callan nuzzles his face against my neck. "For what?"

"For making me happy and giving me a life I could only dream of having. More importantly, for loving me."

Kissing the spot below my ear, Callan tightens his hold on me. "Thanks for letting me make you happy. For letting me give you the life you deserve. I love you, Denver Hawk."

Lightning Source UK Ltd.
Milton Keynes UK
UKHW020738260422
402079UK00010B/927